I0524705

HEARTS AFLAME

FORGED IN THE CITY

A.D. ELLIS

1

GABRIEL "GABE" STERLING

"Is your name really Murder?" I asked the gruff-looking, silent man working on a motorcycle at Whitfield's Motorcycle Sales and Service. I'd heard him referred to as Murder at a recent Christmas party and it had definitely piqued my interest. I was nervously waiting on Bay and the others to arrive. "Of course, it's not, right? I mean, would a parent actually name a baby Murder? Would the hospital even allow that?"

Murder's chest expanded as if he was taking deep breaths as his eyes slid to mine, but he kept working. Silently.

I was likely more talkative than normal because of an off-the-charts level of anxiety. Bay had offered me the apartment above his shop. I really wanted the place. The rent was ridiculously low and it was the perfect size. However, at the Christmas party when Ginny had introduced me to him, I'd soon realized *who* Bay was married and related to, and that was the reason for *the others* coming over before I signed any paperwork on the apartment.

"Sorry, I talk a lot when I'm nervous. And I'm nervous." I fluttered my hand in the air as if it would excuse my word vomit. "Is Murder the name you like best? If I end up living here, I'll see you a lot, right? I don't want to call a guy Murder if he'd rather be called John or something. Murder seems like one of those names that a person would rather maybe leave behind. But I'll call you whatever you prefer." I paced the shop floor and wished Bay and company would show up so I could get this over with. I had a feeling I *wouldn't* be living in this apartment, despite how much I'd *love* to, and I'd rather just get home to my current—but very temporary— apartment and start looking for something else I could afford before my roommate and her new husband kicked me out.

Murder straightened up from the work he was doing on the bike and crossed his arms over his chest. "If I tell you my real name, will you stop talking?" His face didn't break from the scowl it wore, but I saw an interesting curiosity in his brown eyes.

I grimaced. "Maybe? I can't make promises. But I'll try to stop talking about names."

He sighed and rolled his eyes. "My real name is Danny. *Not* Daniel. Daniel was my father's name. He wasn't a *bad* guy, just not someone I want to be named after." He raised a brow as if waiting to see if I'd accept the information or press for more.

I bit my lip and tried to stay quiet. "But where did Murder come from? Were your parents happy with their kid having a nickname like that? Seems like a pretty heavy nickname for a kid." I knew I was rambling.

He closed his eyes and ran a hand over his face. "What time is Bay supposed to be here? Shouldn't he be here by now?" He glanced around the shop as if hoping his boss would suddenly appear.

"I was early. Should be here in a few." I paused and watched him, waiting to see if he'd give me any more info.

"My parents were murdered in a robbery gone bad at the very end of my junior year of high school. I moved from Martinsville to Plainfield to live with a very angry and mean uncle. My last name is Murdoch; the play on words and the rumor that I'd murdered my parents followed me. The nickname stuck. Doesn't bother me too much. Easier to just let people call me what they want than trying to explain it or ask them to call me Danny." He shrugged

I frowned. "I'm so sorry to hear about your parents. Why in the world would anyone think *you* murdered them? That's terrible." I'd be honest, the guy *looked* mean. Big, brooding, short dark hair, tattoos. But that didn't make him a murderer at seventeen.

He rolled his shoulders. "I was in the house when it happened. When the neighbor reported the gun shots, the police arrived, and found me hiding. They questioned me. News travels fast in a small town and isn't always accurate. The rumor started and took off like wildfire. People talk, so it followed me to my uncle's place. He didn't do anything to stop it, so I just dealt with it. Like I said, just easier."

"Well, I will *not* call you Murder. You are Danny to me, now and forever." I drew an X over my heart.

My heart fluttered when Danny bit back what appeared to be an *almost* smile. "Thanks. I'll answer to either."

I checked the time on my phone. One minute until the big reveal. Would we speak here in the shop? An office? I wiped my sweaty hands on my jeans. "Do you work here daily?"

Danny nodded. "Pretty much. I took six months off. Traveled around. Needed to clear my head. Had some money saved up."

"Did it work?" I chewed the inside of my cheek.

"What?"

"Clearing your head?"

He smirked. "Jury is still out. I work mostly every day, but my hours are flexible. I come in when I want or when I have appointments." He ran a hand over his black, buzzed hair. "You planning to be here yapping my ear off every day if you get the apartment?"

I laughed. "Don't sound so excited." A bit of giddiness over the possibility of seeing and talking to Danny that often floated through me. "I work three twelve-hour days a week with an extra short shift or two thrown in from time-to-time. So, you won't have to deal with me *all* the time." I winked. And then had to fight back a smile when Danny seemed to get flustered.

The door opened and four men walked in. All the mechanics stopped what they were doing and hollered hello or gave a wave. As the foursome made it to the back where Danny and I were, Bay smirked and widened his eyes as he approached.

"Ah, I see Murder's being a gracious host and keeping you company?" Bay slapped Danny on the shoulder. "Good to see you, man. Really glad you're back."

"He prefers Danny, I think," I interjected and inwardly rolled my eyes. Yeah, correcting my potential landlord was a great way to get an apartment. "We've just been chatting."

Bay raised a brow. "Sorry, man, I thought Murder was fine."

Danny shot me a look and shrugged. "Danny or Murder, either is fine."

"Danny it is then," Bay answered before turning my way. "You and Danny have been *chatting*? That's a major new development. Danny doesn't do a lot of talking. To anyone."

My cheeks pinked. "I guess I was talking a lot and kinda forced him into it."

Danny chuckled but didn't disagree.

One of the other three guys with Bay cleared his throat. "Wondering if we could get on with whatever this is?"

My stomach flip-flopped. "Sorry, I don't want to take up your time. Should we talk here?"

"Office won't fit all five of us. If you're okay with here, I'm good." Bay gestured toward the repair floor. "Most of them have music playing or earbuds in, we can talk pretty much privately."

Danny took that moment to return to work on the bike in his bay. I watched his tall frame bend slightly as I studied his tattoos, the fluid movement of his muscles under his stained, white work shirt, and his muscular thighs straining against his blue jeans. He wasn't a super beefy guy, more tall and lean, but he had a lot of muscle definition.

"This is my husband, Kyson. He runs Mass. Ave.

Healing Massage. These are his cousins, Bode and Benji Silver. Guys, this is Gabe Sterling, he's thinking about renting the apartment." Bay made introductions, we all shook hands, and then he gestured toward me as if letting me know it was my turn to speak.

I moved away from Danny's workspace and leaned on the half wall that divided part of the repair floor from the stairs and entrance to the apartment. "I'm sure you all are wondering why the heck I asked that you be here before Bay and I discussed me renting the apartment." The guys all nodded, Bode looking the most menacing with a scowl, while Benji and Kyson just looked curious. I took a deep breath and continued. "My mother died the month before I graduated from four years of nursing school. She'd kept my father's identity from me my entire life. I mostly accepted it and never asked. It was the hardest when kids would make fun of me for having no dad."

All four men stared at me with various reactions ranging from *Why are you telling us this* to *Man, that sucks, I'm sorry*.

"Mom got breast cancer when I was in high school, but she refused treatment. It was a very slow growing cancer and I was lucky to have several years with her before she died. A month before college graduation, she held my hand and told me the story of how she got pregnant with me." I paused and took a moment to gather my thoughts.

Bode's scowl deepened.

Benji looked curious.

Kyson appeared sympathetic.

Bay was possibly a combination of all three.

"Mom was a waitress at a bar in Indianapolis before I was born. She met a man and fell hard for him. He'd come to the bar every time he was in town. She said he was the perfect gentleman. Kind, caring, bought her things. Eventually, he put her up in an apartment and promised he'd marry her as soon as he could. Within a year, she was pregnant with me and he was no closer to marrying her than when they first met. She kept her pregnancy a secret for a few months and began badgering him about marrying her." I chewed on a fingernail. "He blew up during one of their fights and admitted that he was married with children who were around twelve years old."

At this point, Bode's face was fiery red, Benji looked resigned, and Kyson had closed his eyes as if he knew what was coming. In fact, all three of the Silver boys seemed to know where this story was going. Was that good? Bad? I had no clue. So, I just continued.

"She broke down and told him she was pregnant. He flipped out and gave her money to get an abortion. The night he left her, he gave her seven thousand dollars to get the procedure, get a new place, and keep quiet about their relationship. She moved in with her mother in a cute little house outside of the city, had me, and never contacted him again. No matter how many times I'd ask about my father growing up, she always promised that she loved me and that was all that mattered." I glanced at each man. "Before she died, she finally gave me his name. I found him online, contacted him, and invited him to my graduation. Mom had passed by then; I likely wouldn't have invited him if she'd been alive, I wouldn't have wanted to upset her."

The guys' eyes all grew wide.

"He was very curt in the phone call, but actually showed up at my graduation. Keep in mind, I'd watched my mom die and just wanted someone to call family. I was so damn lonely growing up, always longing for a brother or sister. I guess I had this misguided hope that he'd be proud of me or something."

Bode snorted.

Benji elbowed him.

Kyson looked sad.

"He showed up. Sneered when he realized I was gay *and* graduating with a degree in nursing. He met me after the ceremony. Told me my sexuality was a 'mistake', but he could get past it. However, he deemed my nursing degree a complete waste. Said if I ever decided to go into something worthwhile, to contact him. Told me that he didn't have time for another child to throw away their life." My eyes stung with the pain of reliving that moment. I'd only hoped for some acceptance and support, instead I got a double whammy of bigotry and complete disinterest. "I've spent the three years since graduating digging to find out all I could about my father and his *real* family." My heart hurt to think that my father had *real* sons but didn't want to know me.

Bode finally cleared his throat. "Which Porn Brother was it?"

I frowned. Not the question I was expecting. "Um, what?"

"The Porn Brothers. Dick and Rod Silver. Total porn star names. Which one was it? I'm guessing Dick, but could just as easily have been Rod." Bode crossed his arms over his chest. He looked pissed and threatening, but I got the distinct feeling it wasn't aimed at me. It was almost as if he was angry on my behalf and wanted to protect me.

"Um, Richard Silver is the name Mom gave me," I mumbled.

Bode scoffed.

Benji rolled his eyes.

Kyson just shook his head.

Bay stared wide-eyed between me and the other guys.

"Dick is our dad," Benji said and pointed between Bode and himself. "We're twins. Kyson is our cousin; his dad is Rod."

"I'm so sorry for this whole situation," Kyson spoke. "I'm sorry for your loss, I'm sorry for you growing up without a father, and I'm sorry that one of the Porn Brothers is your dad. They aren't the greatest guys in the world."

"So, why did you want to tell us this?" Bode scowled.

I shrugged. "I figured out that Bay and Kyson were married. I didn't want to move into a place *knowing* I was your illegitimate brother and then have it come out later. Didn't want to seem like I was hiding anything from you." I bit my lip. "I get if you want nothing to do with me. I didn't tell you this in hopes of gaining a family, I've been fine alone for twenty-five years. I just didn't want it to seem like I was trying to pull one over on you. Mom always taught me to tell the truth first." I chuckled with no humor. "Which is ironic when she wouldn't tell me about my dad, but I guess she knew he wasn't a person I needed in my life." I looked all of them in the eye. "I will understand if you don't want me to rent the apartment; if it's just easier to not have me around. I'd imagine it's kinda difficult to find out your dad isn't the guy you thought he was."

Bode scoffed. "Believe me, what you've told us is

nothing we didn't already suspect of our dear father. He's an asshole through and through. He's never completely accepted our sexuality, but he's actually always been more disappointed in our career choices—especially mine. He sat around like a damn dog hoping to gobble up crumbs when I first opened The Salty Lizard. Used to dangle the money he'd loaned me over my head as a way to control my business decisions. Once I got a bank loan and bought him out, I moved on as a successful businessman and never once tossed him another look."

"Always thought my art studio was a waste of time and talent," Benji added.

"My uncle and my dad think I could have done *so much more* than run a successful massage therapy business," Kyson said with a curl of his lip.

"Damn, sometimes I forget just what assholes your dads are." Bay grimaced and kissed Kyson's cheek. "Sorry," he glanced at me.

"So, you'd be okay with me living here? I promise I wouldn't bother you or try to worm my way into your family." My heart pounded with the hope of landing the apartment.

Bode smirked. "We're completely fine with you living here. If for some reason it doesn't work out, Sage and I have a room you can rent. And, don't even think that you aren't family; no more using the word *illegitimate* either. You're our brother, you're one of us. Hell, even your last name is freakishly close to ours. Sterling and Silver?" He shook his head. "Weird."

I smiled and swallowed a lump in my throat. "Mom said she always wrote their name in doodles. *Mr. and Mrs. Richard Sterling-Silver*. She would have been Violet Sterling-

Silver." I wasn't letting myself think too much about Bode's insistence that we were all brothers now. I'd wanted siblings my entire life. I couldn't allow myself to get too excited about it just yet. Maybe once the shock wore off, maybe once they realized I was just a bastard from their asshole father's cheating, maybe then they'd turn me away. But if I could have the apartment, I'd be happy.

Bode, Benji, and Kyson all gave me hugs. *Hugs*. I could barely believe it. They promised we'd all do a big group meet up soon. And then they left so Bay and I could do the apartment paperwork.

As he headed to his office to grab the papers before taking me upstairs to see the place, I heard a low whistle from my left.

I turned to see Danny, wrench in one hand, towel in the other, staring at me wide-eyed. "Sorry, didn't mean to eavesdrop. I only heard bits and pieces, but you've got almost as crazy of a story as me."

My face heated and I shrugged.

"They're all amazing guys. The Silver crew takes care of their family, blood or chosen. You're in good hands." He gave the tiniest of smiles and a nod and went back to work as Bay returned.

"Ready to see the apartment?" he asked and gestured toward the stairs.

We spent the next forty-five minutes checking out the apartment, discussing rent, and signing paperwork. Bay grilled me and made me sign permission for a background check, but I knew he wouldn't find anything damning. He must have known the same because he said I could move in as early as the next day.

After saying goodbye to Bay, I turned a broad smile toward Danny who was in the process of cleaning up and organizing his work area. "I got the apartment."

Danny smirked—something that I decided was quickly going to be a favorite thing to see—and rolled his eyes. "Oh great. I've got my own little magpie." But he winked as he went about straightening up his tools. "Congrats. Guess I'll see you soon then."

I nodded and gave him a smile and a wave.

I should have been over the moon to have an apartment and three family members who didn't toss me on my ass the moment they heard my story. And I was, believe me, I was definitely thrilled.

But a strange fluttering went through me at the thought of seeing Danny on a somewhat regular basis. *Damn, dude. Chill out. It's been a while for you, I get it. But you don't even know if he's gay*. I rolled my eyes at myself. I'd dated pretty seriously in college, but we broke up shortly after when I got obsessed with finding my brothers. I went on a few dates here and there and a few hookups from time-to-time, but mainly it was just me and my hand these days. True, I didn't know if Danny was gay. But the glances he was sending my way earlier didn't give off a completely straight vibe.

If anything, maybe I could get a new friend. I wouldn't mind that at all.

2

DANNY "MURDER" MURDOCH

Holy shit.

I flopped onto the loveseat in my apartment and ran a hand over my face. After Gabe left the shop, I finished up, came home, and showered. Ready to relax for the evening, I popped open a beer and took a long swig.

My mind went right back to the same thoughts that had been swirling in my head since earlier. Actually, some of them had been present since I caught a glimpse of Gabe at the Silvers' Christmas party.

One, the kid was drop-dead gorgeous. Those blue eyes and that smile were both killer. His hair was dark and thick; he had that messy look that almost appeared to be *fuck it*, but it totally worked for him. Shorter than me and much *softer* looking, he was the perfect height and build to tuck under my arm to cuddle and protect.

As if, Murder. I rolled my eyes. I'd known I was gay since high school, since before my parents were killed. Never told them. After they died, I knew better than to tell my uncle. Uncle Greg was *not* the most welcoming, accepting, understanding man. Hell, he wasn't even bordering on *nice*.

I kissed one guy in high school and threatened to kill him if he told anyone. The nickname *Murder* did come in handy at times.

I didn't tell anyone about my sexuality. I wasn't much of a talker, kept to myself, and didn't have many friends. Hell, Bay was probably the closest thing to a *friend* I had, and he was my boss.

Yeah, I had a handful of hookups in my past, but the people I worked with didn't need to know I was gay. As far as the guys I'd had sex with, they could think whatever they wanted about me. Most people did, pretty much always negative, and I'd learned to just live with it. No use to argue it.

My thoughts circled back to Gabe. I'd heard him say he was a nurse. Why the hell did I find that sexy as hell. I wondered briefly what his ass would look like in a pair of low-slung scrub pants. Did that dark hair cover his chest? Licking my lips, I imagined a dark trail of hair down his stomach disappearing under his waistband. I growled and took another swallow of beer.

I smiled softly, still not able to turn my thoughts to anything else. Damn, the kid could *talk*. Maybe because I was so quiet and such a loner, most people got the hint pretty quickly that I didn't really *do* conversation. It wasn't so much that I didn't *want* to talk, just always felt like I didn't really have anything important to say. No one really needed, or wanted, to hear what I had to say. My parents had led me to believe that with their detached parenting style, and my uncle made damn sure I knew it was better for me to be seen and not heard. As long as I was keeping his house clean, his shop running, and the money coming in from motorcycle repairs, he kept me fed, clothed, and sheltered. That was about it.

Uncle Greg was my savior in that he kept me out of the system, but he didn't give me anything more than the bare necessities. After he died, any hope I had of staying to run his shop went up in flames when the bank took his land and everything on it. I had no choice but to leave and find another job. After floating from job to job, never really fitting in, I finally found a place I felt comfortable. Now, at age thirty-five, I knew I'd stay at Whitfield's for as long as Bay would have me.

As I finished my beer, I realized with a shock there was a strange mix of nerves, dread, and excitement swirling through me as I thought of Gabe moving into the apartment above the shop.

It wasn't like we'd see each other on a daily basis, right? I had my job and my routine. Gabe had a very important job. Once the newness of moving in wore off, I figured he'd get into a new routine and the novelty of having me downstairs to yammer to would quickly become a thing of the past. As long as I pretty much stayed quiet and didn't show him any interest, he'd probably get bored pretty fast and move back to his real friends.

Yeah, stay quiet like you did today? And good luck not showing any interest.

I scoffed. I'd talked to Gabe more today than I'd talked in an entire month or more. And it was going to be hard to not show interest when I'd found myself thinking of nothing but Gabe for over an hour.

Okay, new plan. Let the kid talk my ear off if he

wanted. Return the conversation if I had something to say. And any interest I had in him would have to be of the friendly kind only. No way I could even contemplate hooking up with Gabe; he lived in my boss's upstairs apartment. A hookup could end up very awkward for all involved.

I watched some TV for a while, brushed my teeth, set my alarm, and crawled into bed. I'd get up and run, lift weights, and then start my day. If Gabe happened to be around, fine. If not, all the better. I didn't need the distraction. I also didn't need the stupid fluttery hopefulness squirming in my belly. Me and hope never really had a great relationship.

* * *

The next morning, after a mile run and weights, I grabbed a quick shower. Scrambled eggs, bacon, and toast for breakfast, pulled on my work clothes of a white t-shirt and black jeans with black work boots, and headed to the shop to get some time in on my own bike before my first appointment came in. Living just around the corner from Whitfield's was one of the best decisions I'd ever made.

Thirty minutes into my work, I heard footsteps on the stairs.

"Good morning," Gabe announced with a huge smile and wave. "It's move-in day!"

I gave a quick nod, smirked at his enthusiasm, and went back to work. He had moving to do, I had repairs to do. No reason we couldn't both get our work done without bothering each other.

I heard what I assumed was a vacuum cleaner running

upstairs for about thirty minutes. Then things were quiet for about an hour. Had Gabe left through his outside door?

Just as I was finishing up the work on my own bike, Bay came onto the repair floor and Gabe came bounding down the steps.

"Morning," Bay said to us both with a nod and a smile. "Gabe, getting a good start on everything?"

"Definitely." Gabe beamed. "Got everything vacuumed and cleaned up. Whoever lived there before did a great job keeping it nice. I just dusted and used some hot vinegar water to wipe down surfaces."

I smirked. I knew Xan had been living upstairs before he and Chase got their own place. Wasn't surprised Xan didn't trash the place; seemed like a good guy for sure.

"Xan took great care of the place. I'm glad it's working out for you. You have a lot of stuff to move in?" Bay asked.

Gabe shook his head. "Not too much. Going to go load my car now. Should have it all moved in before the end of the day."

"Let us know if we can help."

My head jerked to look toward Bay. *Us*?

Bay twisted his lips as if trying not to smile. "Was coming to tell you, your first appointment canceled. You've got some free time. Figured you'd want to keep busy and wouldn't mind helping Gabe."

I ground my teeth together. *Damn it*. "Yeah, sure. No problem."

"Really? That would be awesome. Want to ride with me and help me load my car? May take a couple trips, but no one is home at my old place and I was kinda wondering how I'd get some of the heavier things down." His blue eyes sparkled and looked so damn hopeful.

I gave Bay a look. He quickly turned to leave, but not before I saw the shadow of a smile. "Let's get to it then."

Fuck. How in the hell had this happened? I'd gone from keeping to myself and just letting the kid blabber to climbing into his car to spend a few hours helping him move.

"Thanks so much for this. I'll totally pay you for your help," Gabe yammered as he pulled his car onto the street.

"Don't need payment. Just helping."

"Well, how about payment in pizza and beer for dinner?" He glanced my way with a smile.

"Do I seem to be the type of person who can be paid off with pizza and beer?" I tried to keep a straight face, but the look of worry that filled his face had me dropping the mask and giving him a bit of a smile. "Fine, pizza and beer sound great."

We chatted for the twenty minutes it took to drive to Gabe's old place. Okay, correction. *Gabe* chatted for the twenty minutes it took us to get to his old place. I nodded, grunted, and threw in the occasional *yeah* as he talked. How could one person have so many words?

My hand shot to his knee as we pulled up to the apartment. *What the actual hell was I doing*?

Both of us stared at the contact.

What the hell had made my hand grab his damn knee? And why was I now squeezing it? "You nervous?"

Gabe made a garbled sound, cleared his throat, and squeaked, "What?"

Without removing my hand—why the hell was I not moving my hand?—I ran my thumb over his soft jeans.

"You said you talk a lot when you're nervous. Is this nervous chatter or normal chatter?"

Gabe's cheeks pinked and I had to force myself not to wonder if other parts of him would look so delicious all flushed with heat.

"Oh, um," Gabe stammered. "This is mainly normal chatter I guess. I mean, you do make me pretty nervous, but I like you and just like to talk. I'm sorry, I can try to reel it in." He glanced back to my hand on his knee.

"No, you're fine. I just don't want you to be nervous." I gestured toward my hand on his knee. "Sorry for that. I'm not trying to make a move or anything. Promise." I slowly removed my hand and reached for the door handle while trying to dismiss the fact that I immediately missed the contact.

"I wouldn't mind," Gabe murmured.

I nearly gave myself whiplash turning to look at him. "Huh?"

Gabe's eyes were full of mischief and he raised a shoulder. "Just letting you know, I'm single. I would really like to have you as a friend because I have very few of those these days." His gaze fluttered down to where my hand was on the seat before looking back up to meet my eyes. "I'm completely good with friends with benefits if that's something you'd be interested in." His eyes grew wide. "Holy shit, did that just make me sound like the biggest slut ever or what? I'm sorry. I dated a guy for most of college. When we broke up, he took most of our friends with him. I've had some hookups and a few dates, but I'm pretty sure my flirt mode has gone haywire. I'm not asking you to jump me—I mean, if you wanted to, I wouldn't say no, but I'm not expecting it—and it's probably hella weird to have a guy you just met offering a friends with benefits situation. It's weird, right? Totally weird. I mean, I'm serious about friends with benefits, that's definitely still on offer…"

Launching myself over the console, I cupped his face and pressed my mouth against his. Gabe gasped and opened just enough for me to slide my tongue between his plump lips. He tasted sweet and his soft mouth was something I wouldn't mind spending a lot more time exploring. But I pulled away, breathless. "Guess I found one way to get you to stop yammering," I whispered.

What the actual fuck was I doing?

"Wow," Gabe said on a long sigh. "Do I get kissed like that every time I talk too much? If so, I'll have to gather up new topics to ramble about."

We were still only inches apart, our eyes locked.

"I'm really sorry, I definitely should *not* have done that," I mumbled.

Gabe smiled, his eyes sparkling, and he leaned in to brush his lips over mine. "I don't know, I think it was kinda amazing." He deepened the kiss.

Ignoring the part of my brain screaming at me to stop, I moaned into the kiss and enjoyed the hot slide of his tongue against mine. When Gabe whimpered against my lips, my dick pressed painfully against my zipper, and I broke contact.

"Aside from kissing, shoving a dick in my mouth is also a sure-fire way to shut me up." Gabe pecked my lips. "Just so you know," he quipped with a smile and a wink.

I groaned.

"What? I'm just sayin'. I don't see anything wrong with friends with benefits as long as we're open and honest. I'm not against a relationship—let me know if you know of anyone looking for something more serious —but sex with a friend can be great. At least it seems like it could be. I've never had sex with a friend. My best friend in high school was a girl. And a lot of my college friends were girls. The one guy friend I had was definitely *not* my type." He paused for a breath. "Maybe you don't consider me a friend, but I can tell we're going to get along just fine. I want to be your friend no matter what; you don't have to give me dick to have me as a friend. But I'm on board if we want to include some sexual tension relief in our friendship." He winced. "The only thing I'd ask is that we be exclusive. I know, I know, that doesn't sound very casual. But my last boyfriend cheated and I don't think I can handle that. I'd promise to keep things casual and not be clingy, but just no sex with others for as long as we keep our little setup going. If we get to a point where it's just not working for us, we're honest and talk about it." He paused as if waiting for me to respond, but then gasped, "Oh! One other thing. I'm kinda a touchy-feely person. Like I love to hold hands and cuddle. So, there it all is. My offer and my issues. What do you think?"

I stared at him for what seemed like hours. "I think you have *so* many words. Kissing you was great. I don't have a lot of hookups and don't date. Part of me wants to say hell yeah to the offer. The more rational side of me thinks it's a huge mistake. You're related to my boss. You live where I work. If things go south, it could get all kinds of awkward."

Gabe climbed out of the car and gestured for me to follow. "We need to get these things moved before I lose my muscle guy. I can see what you're saying and you've got valid points."

My heart sank a bit as the cold air bit at my face. Maybe I'd protested too much. Hell, it wasn't a good idea, but I wasn't ready to write off his suggestion just yet. My dick protested behind my jeans.

"*But*," Gabe continued, "I say we do the friends thing for a while and just let the *benefits* part be hanging out, touches, and kisses. We're grown men, we can control our urges, right? We'll know if we want to take things farther." He unlocked his door and gestured me inside. After closing the door, Gabe took my hand and pressed himself against me. "I miss touching and kissing *sooo* much. Random hookups aren't good for that. There's something between us, I swear there is and there's no way you don't feel it too. I've never in my life propositioned a friend, especially one I basically just met, for casual sex. That would have been so creepy to me. But with you? There's like this weird draw. We're about as opposite as two people can be, but it's like we click. Okay, maybe that's just wishful thinking on my part…"

I pushed Gabe against the wall and kissed him, hard. Rocking my hips against his, I dipped my tongue deep and devoured his mouth. When we broke apart, I leaned my forehead against his. "Let's just get you moved. Pizza, beer, friendship. I'm on board. If more happens, I'm okay with it. But I think you're lonely and desperate right now. Let's see how you're feeling about me after we spend more time together."

Gabe's eyes softened. "I am lonely. I do want friends. But please don't ever think someone would have to be desperate to want you—either as a friend or a sexual partner." He caressed the side of my face and I shocked myself by leaning into his touch. "At least tell me the truth, do you feel some kind of weird connection between us? I swear I don't do this with every guy who helps me move boxes."

I closed my eyes. Did I feel drawn to Gabe? Hell, yes. I sighed. "Yeah, I feel it. But it's probably just because you're one of the first people to ever give me a second glance—either as a friend or something more. I've had a few hookups, but it's mainly just me and my right hand."

"Mmmm, I'd love to hear more about your jackoff sessions," Gabe murmured and rocked against me. "Also, I'm offended you think that wanting me is only the result of being lonely and horny."

"That's not what I meant," I sputtered.

Gabe winked. "I know. I'm teasing. Let's get things moved."

As we began to tape and stack boxes, he got strangely quiet, only speaking to give directions on what to carry to the car. By the time we had everything loaded—surprisingly, we fit it all in one trip—I was wondering if something was wrong.

"Hey, you good?" I asked as we headed back toward the shop.

He glanced my way, biting his lip, and smiled sadly. "Yeah, can we talk over pizza and beer tonight? My brain's kinda scrambled right now."

"Sure," I agreed. It was weird to see him go from rambling to almost completely silent.

Gabe chattered a bit as we carried things upstairs, but he was definitely off.

Probably regrets what he offered and is wondering how to take it back.

"Thanks so much for all of your help. Can you do pizza at five? Or would six work better?" Gabe held the door open as I prepared to leave.

"Listen, I really don't need any kind of payment. You're off the hook." I longed to run down the stairs and submerse myself in music and repair work, anything to get my mind off the very ridiculous, very real disappointment I felt. It wasn't at all a surprise that Gabe was having regrets. I should have known better than to let my hopes build.

His face fell. "Oh, I mean, I get if you don't want to come for dinner. But I was really looking forward to it."

I couldn't stand the look of sadness on his face, so I pushed aside the rational part of me saying to just chalk the day up to a very weird interaction, and nodded. "I can be here by six."

Gabe's face lit up.

I headed downstairs with my head spinning. On one hand, I was so damn attracted to him, found it completely crazy to *want* to spend time with him, and looking forward to dinner and whatever this odd friendship could become. But the other part of me was already preparing for disaster and disappointment. I didn't really do the friends thing. I had no clue how. And friends with benefits—while my libido was definitely on board—seemed like it could get very murky, very quickly if feelings got involved. I was good at keeping feelings at bay, but I clearly struggled with a lot of my *normal* when it came to Gabe. What if we messed things up and I lost a friend? When in my entire life had I been all that concerned about losing a friend? Had to *have* friends to lose them.

I ran a hand over my face. How did one guy have me so tied in knots?

Maybe it would all be over before it even got started once we talked over dinner. It was probably for the best. But damn, I'd *never* be able to forget those kisses.

3

GABE

I sat on the couch berating myself for my stupidity.

Could I have possibly come across any more desperate?

Fuck.

I found Danny incredibly attractive. But I'd never offered friends with benefits to any other guys I found attractive. So, what the hell was I thinking in this situation?

Yeah, I was more alone now that I moved to a new place. And I was feeling all sorts of anxiety over my dad and my new brothers. Sure, I hadn't had sex in quite a while. Yes, I missed having a boyfriend. But even with all of that, it seemed ludicrous for me to basically offer my ass to this guy I barely knew.

Then I thought of his scowl and *tough* aura, the way his eyes grew wide when I rambled, the little smiles he tried to hide sometimes. The way my belly got all fluttery when I was around him. And that kiss. My God, the man could kiss.

We had very little in common from what I could tell. Okay, we liked pizza and beer. But I was smiley and talkative and did my best to present a happy face. Danny was frowny and quiet and appeared to always be angry. Maybe pensive was a better descriptor.

Why was I so attracted to him? Why was I so determined we'd be friends? Why was I so stupid to throw myself at him?

He kissed you first.

Well, yeah. There was that.

The door buzzed.

Pizza.

I hit the button to let the guy in and headed down the stairs to meet him.

The delivery kid smiled and handed over the two boxes.

I thanked him then nearly dropped the pizzas when Danny stuck his head around the corner as the delivery guy left.

"Hey," he mumbled. "Sorry, didn't mean to scare you."

"No, you're good. Just thought you'd come to the shop side door." I headed up the stairs. Glancing back to make sure Danny was following, I couldn't help the blush that filled my face when I caught him looking at my ass.

Well, that was interesting.

Danny scowled and cleared his throat and climbed the stairs behind me.

I got two beers out of the fridge and handed one to Danny.

"Thanks," he mumbled.

"Get a lot work done today?" I asked as I grabbed paper plates and napkins.

Danny looked shocked by the question. "Um, yeah. Had two appointments and got them all good to go."

"What types of things do people have you do?" I wasn't educated on the mechanics of cars or motorcycles.

He hesitated as if he didn't really understand why I was asking questions. "Oil changes, new tires, spark plugs, new chains. Sometimes rebuild an engine. Sometimes just replace a bulb. Just depends." Danny shrugged and took the plate I handed him. He took three pieces of pizza.

I gestured toward the couch and we settled in with our food and drinks.

"So, you love what you do?" I asked before taking a big, cheesy bite.

Danny finished a bite and took a swallow of beer. "I do. It's all I've done since I was a teenager, so I don't really know much else. Not sure if I'd like something better, but I do love what I do."

"Can you work on cars, too?"

"Yeah, there are some differences, but I can keep a car running with the basics." He shrugged and took another bite.

"That's really cool. I can't change my own oil or a flat tire or anything. Sometimes I feel helpless for not knowing how, then sometimes I think that at least I can help others keep a job by relying on their services." I rolled my eyes. "Basically, I'm clueless and lazy, I guess."

"Nah, some people love it and are naturals. Some people just never get the hang of it. Some people would just rather save the hassle and pay someone else to do it." Danny chewed his lip. "I could teach you how to do your oil if you wanted."

I wrinkled my nose. "Dirty, oily, on my back under a car? No thanks. If I'm going to be on my back under anything, I'd rather be getting dirty in other ways." My cheeks burned and my eyes went wide. "Sorry."

Danny chuckled, a deep gravely sound and I wanted to listen to him do that for the rest of my life. "It's okay."

We finished our pizza and beer. I threw away the plates and put the leftovers in plastic containers in the fridge while Danny tossed the beer bottles.

We wandered back to the couch and sat down, tension thick in the air.

"I need to apologize for the friends with benefits offer," I started.

Danny sighed and nodded as if he'd known that was what was coming. "No worries, I knew you'd realize it was a mistake."

"What? No, not a mistake. I mean, it was rude and way over the line, but I don't regret it in the way you mean. I'd definitely have sex with you, no question. I just hate that I put you in such an awkward situation."

Danny's eyes shot to mine. "Not awkward. A first for me, that's for sure. But I wasn't offended."

"Good to know." I turned on the couch to face him and pulled my knees to my chest. "I've been doing a little self-reflecting. Ever since I was a little kid, I've felt lonely. I'm always the smiley, happy guy, but never have any deep connections. Even turned out my boyfriend wasn't as serious as I'd thought. I longed for siblings growing up. My mom wasn't around as often as she wanted to be because she was working her ass off to keep me fed." I rested my chin on my knees. "Pretty sure I have some daddy issues. At first, because I didn't have a dad and now because I met him and he's a total douchebag prick."

Danny's eyes met mine and softened. He was listening. Not interrupting, not offering answers, just listening.

"I watched my mom die. Even though we both knew it was going to happen, it still sucked. I know she would have been so proud of me earning a full four-year nursing degree. And I'm proud of myself. It was a huge thing to get through college and earn that degree and my license. I *had* to meet my dad or I always would have wondered. But meeting him and finding out that he's an asshole who looks at my birth and all of who I am as a mistake *and* thinks my nursing degree is a waste of time? That was more of a slap to the face than I was expecting." I sighed. "I'm sorry. I didn't mean to trap you here with pizza and unload all of my baggage on you."

Danny smiled softly. "You're fine. I don't mind listening." He chewed the corner of his lip. "Disclaimer, I'm beyond screwed up with my past shit, so I can't promise I'm good at listening or any kind of advice."

I cocked my head and smiled. "I appreciate you listening. If you ever want to talk about your shit, I'm here."

When Danny looked at me like I was crazy, I laughed and continued with my verbal vomit. "I'm so relieved that I've met my brothers. Bode and Benji, even Kyson, seem great, and I'm so grateful they are letting me live here and didn't tell me to get out of their city."

He snorted lightly.

"What?" I frowned.

"Not sure it's *their* city," he said.

"Well, you know what I mean. They could have said no to the apartment, no to eating at their bar, no to being associated with any of their friends or family."

"They could have, but they didn't." Danny's words were quiet. "I've known them for a bit, they are really good guys. I'm sure they will be including you in family stuff before you know it."

I groaned.

"You don't want that?" he asked in surprise.

"I *do* want that. I want to know them, want to know their families. I already know Ginny and Chase—amazing people by the way—and I want to be included. Like, it's all I've ever wanted."

"But?"

"But I don't want to intrude. I don't want them thinking they have to invite me to things and get to know me just because of some sense of loyalty to their father." I ran my hand through my hair.

"I really don't think they'd do that. If they didn't want you in their circle, they'd be polite but distant. I don't see that happening. I think you'll be surprised at how welcoming they are." He shifted on the couch and pulled a leg up under his knee. "Ginny is Chase's aunt, right? How do you know her?"

I smiled sadly. "When I'm not working at the pediatrician's office, I volunteer at Rose Gardens. It's an assisted living center. Ginny is one of the patients."

"She's sick?"

I nodded. "Yeah, she's got cancer. She's not doing chemo and has had quite a few good years, able to spend them with her adopted daughter, find Chase—he's her nephew—and be surrounded by friends and family. But she's well-aware that she's on the last leg of her journey."

Danny frowned. "She's got a daughter? How's she taking care of her?"

"It's kinda a twisty story. Rosie is Chase's little sister. He never knew she was born because he left his abusive mother and joined the Army. Ginny has been Rosie's guardian since her birth. When Ginny was diagnosed, she asked for help with getting Rosie placed with an adoptive family."

"Wait."

I could see the wheels turning.

"Ah, Bode and Sage have a little girl named Rosie. That's Ginny's daughter?"

"Well, niece if we're talking by birth, but yeah."

"Crazy how so many people are connected. Have you heard the story of how Benji and Rhys got together?" Danny smirked. "It's not gossip, promise."

I waggled my brow. "Do tell."

He launched into a story about how my brother, Benji, and Rhys had been casually dating then ended up in some mess up where they both were trying to lease the same building and open competing art studios.

"Wow, that's some drama right there. But they ended up together?" I asked.

"Yeah, together, happy, successful." Danny was quiet for a moment. "That's really sad about Ginny. Is she getting a lot sicker?"

I pursed my lips. "She's been having really good days and really yuck days."

"You like volunteering there?"

"Yeah, it's good. I love the older people. They've got

amazing stories." I smiled as I thought of the sassy, funny, dear clients I got to spend time with a couple times a week if my schedule allowed.

"Why not be a nurse there?" Danny shifted on the couch and I didn't miss the fact that he moved slightly closer to me.

"I love kids. They are cute and funny. Don't get me wrong, I really enjoy the elderly too. But kids are usually just beginning their lives and it's not as often that you lose a child. I think I love volunteering with the older folks because I can just listen and spend time with them and don't have to be *as* concerned with their medical prognosis."

"God, I bet it sucks when a kid is really sick," Danny's voice was gruff.

I smiled sadly. "Yeah, we see some rough cases. Honestly, I think certain pediatric specialties at a hospital would be too much for me. At the pediatrician's office, I usually only have to deal with shots and flu and maybe some rashes and broken bones. Every so often we deal with something more serious, but then it's often sent on to a specialist."

Danny's eyes grew wide. "Oh my God, do you have to give little kids their shots?"

I chuckled. "Yep. The doctors usually have the nurses do it so they aren't the bad guys." I nudged him with my foot. "Don't worry, I'm an expert. I can usually distract or do it so quickly that there are barely any tears. Honestly, a lot of times the parents make it worse than the kids do."

Danny winced. "Damn, man. I can't imagine shoving a needle into baby flesh."

I cackled. "God, that makes me sound so evil."

"Shots suck. I hate even getting a flu shot."

I raised my brow. "Yet, you've got more than one tattoo." I was curious where all of his tattoos were located and if I'd ever get to see them.

Danny shook his head. "Tattoos are different. The needles are barely puncturing the skin, not going in deep, not putting medicine in. Plus, the tattoo is something pretty to look at later. A shot just gets you a bloody bruised bump."

I laughed. "Come into the office for your next flu shot. I'll go in easy." I winked. "May even give you a band-aid for your boo-boo." I wasn't sure if the innuendo was blatant enough, but the way Danny's cheeks pinked, I assumed it was.

We spent another hour or so chatting. I couldn't get over how easy it was to just hang out and talk with him. Yeah, maybe I did the majority of the talking, but Danny seemed to be enjoying himself. I definitely didn't get any bored and annoyed vibes from him.

I yawned and checked the time. "Shit, I hate to be the party pooper, but I've got three twelves coming up so I've got to get some sleep."

Danny's eyes widened. "Oh man, I'm so sorry for staying so long." He stood up quickly.

"No, no. Don't worry. I'll always say when I need to get to bed. It's a bummer, but the schedule is pretty great when I'm not working." I stood and took his hand as we walked toward the door.

Danny glanced down at our joined hands.

"Sorry, touchy-feely, remember? I had to control myself from cuddling on the couch." I shrugged and leaned my head on his shoulder.

"I wouldn't have cared," Danny spoke softly and I grinned.

Once we reached the door, I turned to face him and didn't let go of his hand. Enjoying the warmth and the way our fingers entwined just right, I mumbled, "I really am sorry for putting you on the spot with the whole friends with benefits thing, but I'm *not* going to take it back. I want us to be friends and if we find that we want more than that, cool. If not, that's fine too. Friends, sex, more, less, I don't really care as long as I can feel this connection. It's been a very long time since I've felt connected to someone—and I've got to be honest, I've *never* felt this weird, intense connection to others like I feel with you—and I don't want to lose that."

Danny stared at our hands before looking up to meet my eyes. "I'm not good at friendships," he grumbled and my heart hurt for him. "Not because I don't want friends, I've just never really had any. My past, the nickname, all of it just makes it hard to make friends. People are scared of me or think that I'm an asshole or mean. I really just don't have a lot to say." He took a deep breath. "I'm totally willing to give friendship a shot." He smirked when I pouted my lips out. "I'm not saying no to the benefits part, but let's not force it. We'll do the friends thing and see what happens from there. That okay with you?"

"That sounds perfect to me." I leaned up on my toes and brushed a kiss against his cheek, then his chin, and hovered over his mouth to whisper, "I think a sweet goodnight kiss needs to happen from here."

Danny smiled and closed the space between us to capture my mouth in a soft kiss laced with heat and promise. "If friendship means kisses like this all the time, I'm in." He winked.

"Could mean kisses that are a lot *more* than this. Plus, *other* activities." I kissed him again and threw my arms around him to hug him close. "But we'll have to see if those things just happen on their own. You know, wouldn't want to force anything." I rocked my hips against his and chuckled when he groaned.

"Give me your phone number?" Danny whispered at my ear.

Once we exchanged numbers and said goodbye, I showered and headed to bed. Three twelves were great in that they gave me a lot of time off during the week, but by the third evening, I'd be dragging ass for sure.

* * *

Three days later, I dragged my tired ass up the stairs feeling every single one of the thirty-six hours I'd worked. But I smiled at the thought of how fun it had been to text and flirt with Danny during my breaks at work and before crashing in bed each night.

When my phone rang, I startled.

Danny.

I answered with a smile. "Hey."

"You home?"

"Yep, gonna shower and die in bed." I kicked my shoes off.

"Okay, won't keep you long. Just wanted to be sure you were home."

My smile was ridiculous and I felt all gooey. "Hey, before I go, tomorrow is Saturday. Are you available?"

"Depends who's asking." I heard the smirk in his words.

"Well, there's this really hot, sexy nurse who is new to Mass. Ave. and he was wanting to walk around and check out the shops and maybe grab lunch. Interested?"

"Hot, sexy nurse? Hmmm, I don't know. I've sort of got this thing slash not-a-thing with a friend. Kinda a friends with benefits thing, kinda not. Not sure I should go walking Mass. Ave. with a hot, sexy nurse."

"Holy shit, that may be the most words you've ever strung together," I teased. "I bet your friend would love to go walking with you. Maybe you should take him instead of the sexy nurse."

"How about I take the friend who *is* a hot, sexy nurse. Win-win."

"Perfect. As long as I get to pick where we eat." I turned the phone to speaker and stripped from my scrubs.

"Wouldn't have it any other way," Danny said. "Sleep well. Text me when you're awake tomorrow. I'll come over."

"Or, I could come see where you live," I suggested.

"Is that something friends do?" Danny asked.

I grinned. "It's definitely a benefit to friendship."

"Okay, tell me when you're awake and I'll give you my address. G'night."

"Night," I murmured and disconnected.

I swear, I couldn't have been more exhausted, but I floated through my shower and fell to sleep with a huge smile.

* * *

The next morning, I bounded out of bed and texted Danny.

Me: *Can I come over around ten thirty? We'll walk Mass. Ave. and then figure out lunch?*

Danny: *Yep, sounds good.*

He sent me his address and I smiled as I brushed my teeth and climbed into the shower. When I got out, I wrapped a towel around my waist and eyed the lacy underwear in the lingerie bag on my bedroom floor. I needed to do a load of delicates, but I had one other pair I could wear before I *had* to do laundry. I didn't wear the lace *every* day; some days I opted for silk or mesh bikinis, some days cotton boxer briefs, some days I went for a thong. But lace was always an option.

I grabbed the last pair of lace underwear from my drawer and let the soft material slip through my fingers. I adored sexy underwear. The right pair could set the tone for the whole day. I paused before pulling the delicate lace up my legs and over my ass. What would Danny think of a friend—or maybe someday more than a friend—wearing lace underwear?

As the material slid up and over my cheeks, I shrugged and shook my butt in the mirror. If Danny didn't like it, so be it. I wasn't going to change who I was or what I liked for a guy. For anyone. I eyed my nicely rounded ass cupped in a soft yellow lace and smiled as I palmed my long cock tucked snuggly under the material. Who wouldn't think this looked sexy?

I pulled on some worn jeans, a gray Henley, and a pair of sneakers. With a heavy, fleece-lined hoodie tossed over my arm, I was ready for the cold day of wandering my new street. Well, I didn't live exactly *on* Mass. Ave., but I was close enough to it to call it mine. I threw a chapstick in my pocket, grabbed my wallet, phone, and keys, and headed down the stairs through the shop.

Bay looked up from whatever paperwork he was doing in his office. "Morning," he called out.

"Sorry, should have gone out the back, but thought I'd say hi to whoever was working," I blushed.

"Not a problem at all. You heading out?"

"Yeah, Danny and I are going to walk Mass. Ave. and get lunch." I pulled my hoodie on and zipped up.

"Nice day. Cold, but not terrible. And at least the sun is out." Bay smiled as he put away whatever he was working on. "I'm glad you're getting Danny out. He's a great guy, one of my most talented mechanics—and I'm thrilled he's back, but he'd opt to stay in and alone if given the chance. I'm not saying there's anything wrong with being alone or staying in, but I'm glad you guys can buddy up. Have fun." He paused and quirked a brow. "Actually, you may see Xan and Chase out and about. I think they were going to wander around and grab lunch too."

"You have plans today or just working?" I pocketed my wallet in my jeans and slid my keys in my hoodie pocket. I'd text Danny when I left Whitfield's.

"Finishing up this paperwork. Then Kyson and I are taking Cori to my mom's place. She's watching Cori so we can take Arlo to the Children's Museum." Bay smiled and his eyes lit up when he talked about his children. "Probably eat dinner with Mom and Millie later."

"Sounds great. I've heard the Children's Museum is fantastic."

"It really is, you should go with us sometime."

"That would be fun," I answered honestly. I loved kids and I was learning that the Silver crew—both directly related and extended members—really were great people. I knew Ginny spoke very highly of all of them.

"Have fun today," Bay said with a smile and a wave.

I offered polite hellos to all the employees working in the garage and then smiled and waved at the lady organizing the retail shop. Was I just well-rested and excited to be in my new place? Or was I giddy because I was spending the day with Danny? Combination of both probably. Add in the sexy slide of lace against my cock and ass and I was prepared for a very enjoyable day.

Danny smiled when he opened the door. "Good morning."

I bit my lip and tried not to preen as his eyes gobbled me up from head to toe. "Do I get a tour?"

He rolled his eyes. "It's not much different than yours. Small, but it's mine and it's comfy. I love living so close to the shop." He gestured toward the open living room. The place really did resemble my apartment.

"Why didn't you snag the place above the shop?" I wondered aloud.

He shrugged. "Was always someone living there or it was open when I wasn't around. This is fine. Gives me a chance to *leave* work, but still be just around the corner."

"It's really nice. Simple. I can see a lot of you here."

Danny snorted. "Because I'm simple?"

I laughed. "Oh my God, no. Not what I meant. Just nothing too fancy. You're quiet and down-to-earth, that's the feel I get here." I moved closer and wrapped my arms around his waist for a hug.

I loved how Danny—despite still learning of my need for hugs and kisses and trying to figure me out—just held me close while I breathed him deep.

"Mmmm, thanks. Good morning." I kissed his cheek.

"Good morning. You want to head out?" His pink cheeks were absolutely adorable.

"Yep! First stop, coffee shop. Or tea shop because I really want tea, but a coffee shop should work fine. You like coffee? Let me guess. Black?"

Danny smirked. "I don't mind a little cream and sugar, but yeah, I can drink it black."

"You like black, huh? Leather, helmet, bike, jeans, boots. All black."

He shrugged. "It comes with the territory I guess."

We chatted a bit before arriving at The Garden Table. I got the biggest chai latte they had and Danny ordered the same.

"You like chai latte? See, we're meant to be friends." I bumped my hip against his.

He smirked and glanced down at his black Chuck Taylors. "Never tried it. Figured if you liked it, it must be good."

My eyes grew wide. "Oh wow, that's pressure. I mean, I love it. Do you like tea? If you don't like it, I'll buy you a coffee. I mean, I think it's maybe the best hot drink ever, but you may not. You should have asked for a taste of mine first just to see…"

Danny leaned into me and whispered, "Am I going to have to kiss you right here to get you to shut up?"

I clammed my mouth shut and shook my head. As much as I enjoyed Danny's kisses, I wasn't a huge fan of making out in public. "No, I'll stop. I just don't want to be responsible for you not liking your drink."

"You won't be. I made the decision to order it. Plus, if I like it, you can take all the credit." He winked.

"I like the way you think."

When our names were called, we gathered our drinks. I stuck two napkins in my pocket.

"Planning to spill it?" Danny teased.

I pursed my lips. "No, but it's always good to be prepared."

We walked outside and I was grateful for the warm cup in my hands as the winter chill hit my face.

I took a sip of my drink and sighed. "So good." I turned anxious eyes toward Danny and watched as he took a drink.

He licked his lips and took another sip before smiling. "It's good."

"Yeah?" I smiled.

"Really good. I'd definitely drink this any time." He took another drink.

"Yay! Besties should always have a favorite drink." I bumped into him.

Danny gasped and jerked to a stop.

I turned to look at him and realized in horror that I'd made him spill his drink. I ripped a napkin from my pocket and helped him wipe up. "I'm so sorry," I mumbled. "We're not far from your place. Do you need a new shirt? Did it get on your pants? I don't want you sticky all day. Sorry, so sorry," I continued as I took his cup and wiped the excess from it.

"Gabe?" Danny took his cup from me and squeezed my hand.

"Yeah?" I stopped yammering and looked at him.

"I'm fine. I'll just be more prepared the next time you grab napkins. I thought it was *just in case*, I didn't realize I needed to be on guard," he teased, caressed a thumb over my hand, and then dropped it as we began walking again.

We spent the next couple hours popping in and out of fun stores like Pumkinfish, Global Gifts, Decorate, Homespun, Indy Reads Books, and Silver in the City, along with a couple stops at The Best Chocolate in Town and Mass. Ave. Wine.

"One last stop, then let's take this stuff back to my place before we go get lunch." I held up the numerous bags I'd collected throughout our shopping spree. "I swear, if I ever learn to crochet, I'm going back to get a bunch of yarn."

Danny laughed. "I think Vic Black crochets. You know, the guy dating Tyler Gold, Rhys's nephew? I bet he'd teach you."

"Maybe. It looks fun, but I think I just like the yarn the best." I gestured toward Toolbox. "I need an underwear fix."

His cheeks pinked, but he followed.

After twenty minutes, I'd decided on a couple mesh bikinis, a super cute thong, and some tiny, silky shorts. I started to ask the adorable employee if they had any lace options, but decided against it for the time being. Danny already looked as if he was about to swallow his tongue, and I wasn't sure in the middle of a men's underwear store was the place to tell him I liked to wear lace panties.

As we walked back toward my place, Danny glanced at all the bags I carried. He had exactly two purchases. A mystery book he picked up at Indy Reads Books and a little four pack of chocolate. "You like to shop, huh?" His eyes crinkled at the corners.

I blushed and bit the corner of my lip. "Yeah. I don't go often. But these shops were new to me and I just got paid. I may have gone a little overboard, but it was fun, right?"

"Yeah, it was fun to watch you. I'm not sure I'll ever *enjoy* shopping." He followed me up the back stairs. When we reached the door, my hands were full and I couldn't grab my key. Danny leaned in close, took the bags from me, and whispered, "If you ever want to go shopping again, I'll go as moral support and carry your bags."

My heart nearly beat out of my chest. When my hands were free, I threw my arms around his neck. "That's one of the nicest things anyone has ever said to me. Thank you."

Danny's eyes burned into mine.

I wanted to kiss him. Was that too much? Was I pushing too fast?

He took the decision away from me and brushed his lips against mine.

I sighed into the kiss and welcomed his tongue to slide alongside mine.

He broke the kiss first and pressed his forehead against mine. "Why have I wanted to do that all damn day? I'm fucking thirty-five years old. I don't spend all day thinking about kissing. Until you," he huffed.

I smiled broadly. "Proves you needed a friend just as much as I did."

"Not feeling all that friendly toward you right now," he growled and dipped his head to kiss me again.

"If you're lucky, you can be my audience when I model my new underwear," I murmured against his lips.

Danny groaned. "Another benefit to being friends with you?"

I chuckled. "Not all my friends get that benefit. Seems like I've upgraded you to the ultimate package." I fished the key from my pocket and unlocked the door. "In fact, I think I'll go put a pair of these on right now." I winked and pulled an individually plastic-sealed red mesh pair out and waved them around. "I'll be right back."

His eyes nearly bore holes in me when I sauntered back into the living room. "Is it normal to know what underwear your friends are wearing?"

I grinned. "That's part of the ultimate package."

Danny wrapped an arm around my waist and pulled me close. "Does the ultimate package include wanting to strip underwear off your friend with your teeth?"

I moaned into the kiss as he captured my mouth and plunged his tongue deep. *Holy shit*.

He tore himself away from me and took a deep breath. "Sorry, that was too far. I'm sorry."

I stepped closer and ran a hand up his chest. "Don't be sorry. I like you. I'm not saying I want to marry you. I don't even want to get engaged. But I'd love to call you a friend. Hang out, sex, stripping underwear off me with your teeth, I'm down for it all." I kissed him. "We're grown-ups. If we both agree to having fun and seeing where this goes, I say let's do it. We can let it be as casual or as serious as we want." My stomach chose that exact moment to growl. "And now it's time to feed Gabe before he gets super grumpy."

Danny laughed, hugged me close, and kissed the top of my head. It felt a lot more than casual, but I couldn't deny that I loved it. Was I setting myself up for a huge heartache? I shook away the negative thought. I liked Danny. I wanted to spend time with him. I was happy to have him as a friend. The sexual tension and attraction were a bonus and I intended to enjoy it as long as I could.

* * *

We ended up at Fat Dan's for lunch.

"Isn't that Chase and Xan?" I asked as two men walked in and waited to see the host for a seat.

Danny glanced toward the door. "Yeah." He looked around the restaurant. "Should we ask them to join us? It's crowded and we've got a four-top table."

I smiled. Danny didn't always have a lot to say, and he was often scowly, but he had a good heart. I think he *wanted* friends, he just had never been given a chance or the opportunity to build those friendships. "Of course," I answered and stood. "I'll go invite them to our table."

I walked over toward Xan and Chase. We'd only met briefly at the Christmas party, but I figured Xan would at least recognize Danny from the shop. I smiled and waved as they waited their turn to get a table. "Hey guys." I stuck out my hand to shake. "Gabe Sterling. I'm living above the shop. Danny and I have a four-seater, you want to join us? It's pretty crowded and the wait may be a while." I gestured over my shoulder and Danny waved.

Xan smiled and returned the wave.

"That would be excellent. I guess we hit it right at the busy time," Chase said.

We all settled in at the table, greetings were exchanged, and drink orders were placed. Fat Dan's was known for great food and drinks. Once we'd placed our lunch orders, the four of us fell into conversation like we'd been friends for years. Okay, Danny talked a little less than the rest of us, but even he got pretty wordy when Xan brought up a repair he was working on.

Delicious food, great drinks, good conversation, it was so very different than my past friendships and relationships. In the past, everything seemed forced. Or the friends were only there because of the guy I was dating or because they needed me to help them study. I was realizing that a lot of my friendships were very surface and one-sided. The time I was spending with Danny—and even just at lunch with Chase and Xan—felt deeper and more genuine than any relationship I'd ever had in the past. I looked forward to possibly getting to know Bode, Benji, and Kyson better—it felt important to know my actual blood family—but even if I was only ever friends with them in the periphery of their crew, I thought I'd be okay with that as long as I had Danny.

Was I putting too much stock in whatever Danny and I had? Friendship? More? What about when he got tired of my mouth? What if he couldn't accept my desire to wear lace? What if the Silvers decided I wasn't worthy of their friendship and Danny had to choose between Bay—who of course would side with his husband, Kyson—or me? Of course, he'd choose his steady job over some desperate kid he'd just met.

"Hey, where'd you go?" Danny asked and jostled my leg with his hand on my knee.

I pulled myself from the tailspin of negative thoughts and glanced around the table. "Sorry. Zoned out for a little bit." I popped a tater tot in my mouth and tried to smile.

Danny narrowed his eyes as if he didn't believe me. Did he truly know me that well already? He let it go, but I had a feeling he'd bring it up when the others weren't around.

We laughed and chatted as we finished our food. Everyone ordered one more drink and the conversation turned to Chase's aunt.

"Ginny adores you," he stated. "Says it's always a good day when you're on the volunteer list. She said she'd never tell some of the other volunteers, but you're her favorite."

I blushed. "That's sweet. I love hanging out with her. We've been reading some books. She's always fun to chat with; she's got a lot of fun stories."

Chase laughed. "She does. Would've been fun to be a fly on the wall during some of her adventures." He sipped his cider. "Beware. Millie told her she should have you read sexy romance stories to her. I'm pretty sure Millie is looking for some raunchy titles. You've been warned."

I nearly spat out my drink. "Oh my God, I'm not reading sex scenes to old people. I mean, I'm sure they miss sex. And there's nothing wrong with sex. I'm sure the scenes are quite the turn-on. But I can't read them out loud. Just can't. Do you think there are elderly folks sneaking to each other's rooms and getting it on? Oh my God, I'd never even thought of that. I bet they do. I bet there's a lot of kinky old people sex going on after curfew. Now I'm going to constantly be eyeing each resident trying to figure out which ones are sneaking out and getting it on."

Xan and Chase stared at me with wide eyes.

Danny leaned close, a hand gripping my knee again, and whispered teasingly, "Do you need my tongue in your throat to shut you up?"

I clamped my mouth shut and caressed Danny's hand on my knee before he removed it. I instantly missed his touch. "Sorry, I get super chatty sometimes." I knew my cheeks were pink.

Xan laughed. "I don't think I've ever heard that many words from Danny in the whole time I've known him, and you just spewed them all in thirty seconds. You two are the very definition of opposites."

Danny smirked. "As different as night and day." But he cocked his head and studied me. "Maybe a little more in common than we originally thought."

My head spun as I wondered what he was talking about. His wink promised *later* and I took a final sip of my beer.

After paying our bills, the four of us walked out into the bright sunshine and frosty temps.

"We should all grab lunch again sometime," Chase said. "We eat at The Lizard a lot. You guys like it?"

Danny nodded. "It's great. Food is definitely as good if not better than any place in the city. And it's comfortable."

"I love working there. Not planning to work there my whole life, but it's good money, I adore my bosses, and the food is great. I love the regulars." Chase pulled a cap onto his head and down over his ears. "It's fucking cold. Let's get home."

Xan laughed and nudged Chase. "See you guys later. Thanks for sharing a table with us."

As we walked toward home, Danny asked, "What type of movies do you like?"

"I like a lot, but I love comedy and horror." I shoved my hands in the pockets of my sweatshirt.

"Horror? I would have never guessed." He was quiet for a moment. "You want to come watch movies and we'll order in something for dinner later?"

My heart took a flying leap and I bit back a smile. "I'd love that. But I can't stay over. No matter how much you beg and plead, I need to go home. I've got laundry to do tomorrow."

Danny laughed. "I can respect that."

That's how I found myself cuddled under a blanket thirty minutes later with Danny's front plastered to my back as we started our first movie. Despite the creepy plot and the surprises that had me jumping, I realized two things. One, I was sleepy. Two, I was very distracted with Danny pressed against me.

"You tired?" Danny murmured against my ear.

"Mmhm," I answered.

"You can sleep." He brushed his nose along my hairline. "Back there, at lunch, where did you really go?"

I thought through my answer for a moment. "I was thinking about how easy and natural it is to be around you and most of the whole crew—at least those I've met so far. And how none of my past relationships—friends or more—were ever that easy. It was all very surface and one-sided. Maybe not even one-sided. Just not genuine." I clasped his hand and held it to my chest. "What did you mean when you said we had more in common than we first thought?"

Danny squeezed my fingers. "We're very different. That's not in question. But I'm realizing that we both have been lonely. Both looking for friendship—maybe *more* —and didn't even know how much we needed it." He used our joined hands to nudge my face until I turned to meet his. So close I could feel his breath, Danny leaned in and kissed me. He tasted of beer, but also of temptation, promise, and just him. A flavor I was already addicted to. When he broke the kiss, I whimpered, but he just smiled. "Nap for a bit. We can see what feels right when we wake up."

* * *

I woke up toasty warm and comfier than I'd ever been. I shifted and yawned, wiggled against the warmth, and froze.

"Sleep well?" Danny whispered in my ear as he tightened his arm around me and pressed his hard heat against my ass.

I'd forgotten I was asleep with Danny. I loved that I had slept so soundly. I adored having his arms around me. And his arousal turned me on even more. Would it be stupid to act on it? Did he want to do anything about it? Maybe it was just a natural reaction.

"Yeah, slept great." I rolled over in Danny's arms and yelped when he grabbed me to keep me from falling from the couch. Curled against his chest, I felt protected. I felt wanted and confident. "How would you feel about revisiting the whole peeling my mesh underwear off with your teeth?"

Danny growled and devoured my mouth with hot, pressing lips and long, slow thrusts of his tongue. "That's a lot more than kissing. Is it part of the ultimate package?"

I chuckled. "Yes, definitely."

"As long as you're comfortable with it and you don't think we'll mess up our friendship," Danny whispered.

"I'm very comfortable with it. Our friendship means the world to me, but it's not really a normal friendship, you know? We hit it off immediately, I kinda steamrolled you into being my friend, so I'm not sure we can base what happens next on whether or not it's what would normally happen. As long as we're both okay with things and we're only messing around with each other while we're doing this, I'm good with it."

Danny cupped my chin and made me look at him. "And what happens if one of us maybe starts feeling a lot more than friendly toward the other?" He nuzzled his nose against mine.

My heart caught in my throat. Did he already know I was feeling more? Or did he mean *he* was feeling more? Swallowing thickly, I licked my lips. "I think friends who start feeling more than friendly toward each other should give the feelings time to blossom and see where they go. Maybe the feelings mean that they're destined for something more."

He gripped the back of my head and kissed me then. Hard and deep. "I want to take that underwear off you and feel you against me."

Fuck yes.

"I'm game. Get your pants off."

We both shimmied out of our jeans and stripped our shirts over our heads while laughing and desperately trying to keep me from falling off the couch. We sobered quickly when our hot, naked skin connected.

Danny's chest and stomach were covered in a light smattering of dark hair, his dark pink nipples pebbled, his trim waist in the perfect V, and a deliciously plump cock leaking onto the gray of his boxer briefs.

I palmed my dick, the mesh a welcome sensation against my skin. My body heated as he looked me up and down. I knew he saw my smooth chest, light pink nipples, a fine line of hair disappearing under the mesh, and a long cock pressing tightly against the material.

"Gonna have to take a rain check on removing them with teeth. I wanna suck you so badly, but feel like that's a bit much for the first time; if I get my mouth anywhere near your underwear right now, I'm not going to be able to keep my mouth off you." Danny's words were gruff as he kissed my neck, my jaw, my ear.

"Wanna feel you come on me," I whimpered. "Rub off on me."

We stripped out of our underwear in mere seconds.

I shuddered when our cocks connected as we pressed our hips together. "Fuck, oh fuck," I mumbled. I glanced down to where our throbbing cocks met, both of us leaking, his darker and wider, mine a paler pink but just as long as his.

Danny rolled to his back and pulled me on top of him. "Fuck yourself on me," he commanded.

I began to rock my hips and rut my cock alongside his.

His large, hot hands found my ass and held tight. I nearly came right then.

"You feel so damn amazing," Danny murmured against my lips. "Sit up, wanna jack us both."

I shifted to straddle his hips and gasped as he took both shafts in his big hand and began to stroke. "Fuck, Danny. I won't last."

"Good, me neither. Fuck my hand, come for me. Want to see your cum all over me, mixed with mine." Danny continued to stroke, thumbing my slit, smearing our precum, and never taking his eyes from our dicks. "Do it, come for me."

I gave in to the sensation, my balls drawing up tight, a tingle in my spine, and threw my head back as my release shot between us.

Danny moaned and his cock throbbed against mine as he came at the same time.

I collapsed on his chest, breathing hard. "That was great." I kissed his neck. "I mean, it was great for me. Shit, maybe it wasn't great for you. I know I'm probably not the best fuck ever, but it seemed pretty good, right? I mean, you definitely came, you can't fake that. But maybe it wasn't what you wanted? I'm sorry, I…"

Danny gripped my chin and kissed me deeply. When we finally broke apart, we were both breathing heavily again. "It was perfect. Amazing. Best I've ever had."

I smiled and snuggled against him again.

Several moments later, my belly growled.

"Let's wipe up and order food," Danny suggested as he rolled from under me and stood up, reaching a hand down to help me up. "I loved every second of that," he whispered against my mouth, his hand softly cupping my spent dick, "and if the ultimate package allows for it, I'd love to taste you after dinner."

I licked my lips. "So, like I could be dessert?"

Danny smirked. "Something like that."

"I love it." I kissed him. "As long as I get to sample dessert too."

"I think that can be arranged."

We got cleaned up and dressed, then ordered food from The Salty Lizard.

When the knock sounded at the door, I thought Danny was going to burst into flames when he saw Sage on the other side with our bags of food. I guessed he wasn't used to seeing people he knew after having sex with a friend.

I bit my lip and peeked from behind Danny's broad shoulders. "Hi, Sage." I knew I had sex hair and my cheeks were likely as red as a fire engine.

Sage—who was technically my brother-in-law, right?— just smiled and handed the bags over. "Threw in a couple extras, on the house. Enjoy." He turned to leave, but paused and turned back around. "We all need to get together soon. Bode is driving me insane talking about getting to know his little brother."

Danny took my hand and I croaked out a thank you as Sage left.

"You okay?" Danny asked.

"Yeah, just feeling kinda emotional about Bode wanting to know me. If he wants to know me, maybe the others want to as well."

"Bode's the hardest of the bunch in my opinion, so if you can win him over, you're golden." Danny kissed me soundly and then unloaded our feast.

By the time we stuffed ourselves and cleaned up, the

day was close to an end. I caught Danny in the corner between the kitchen counters and wrapped my arms around his neck. "I've got just over an hour and half before I need to head home. Any ideas what we should do with our time?" I kissed along his neck and smiled when he shivered under my touch.

"Movie? Card game? Puzzle?" Danny mumbled against the side of my head.

"Eeww, puzzles? I can't stand puzzles. They make me super anxious and antsy."

Danny laughed. "Okay, so no puzzles. Gotcha."

"What other ideas do you have?" I rocked my hips against his. "Think very carefully about your answer because it *should* involve mesh panties, teeth, and sucking me like a lollipop."

His face was very serious and his eyes full of heat. "I'm down, but I want you on board. The underwear turned me on, I probably shouldn't have said what I did. It was too much and put you in an awkward position."

I cupped his head in both hands and traced his lips with my thumb. "The only thing that's awkward right now is how hard I am and how much I want to swallow your cock, but not until after you suck me off."

Danny choked out a laugh. "Good to know." He kissed me, began to walk us from the kitchen, and didn't even flinch when I hopped up to wrap my legs around his waist. "Bedroom? Couch?"

I bit my lip. "If we go to your bed, I'm going to want to stay there and let you do deliciously nasty things to me." I kissed him and pressed my rock-hard cock into his abdomen. "While that sounds like the perfect way to spend an evening, I really do have stuff I need to do at home."

"That's fine, I don't want to move too fast," Danny murmured against my mouth as he turned toward the couch. "The bed seems a little, I don't know, *more* than the couch."

I leaned back against the cushions with a laugh. "Yeah, because sucking me until I blow down your throat is a lot less intimate on the couch than on a bed."

Danny rolled his eyes. "Yeah, yeah. I know, but the bed is just," he paused with a shrug.

"I've never had a guy in my new bed at my new place," I admitted softly. "So, I get it."

He took a deep breath. "Yeah, same for me. I've never brought a hookup home, so it's all new territory for me."

"Good thing I'm not just a hookup," I quipped and wiggled my hips. "I believe you have some work to do."

Danny grinned, popped the button on my jeans, and slid them down my legs. "Fuck," he growled when the removal uncovered my bulging cock tight behind the red mesh. He pressed kisses along my hip bones, nuzzled his nose against the trimmed pubes behind the mesh, and ran his hot tongue over my aching cock.

"Need you to suck me before I ruin this perfect scene by coming all over myself." I panted out the words as I rocked my hips gently up to meet his tongue.

He nipped at my hip bones, tongued wet kisses along my V-lines, and hooked his thumbs in the band at my waist. He only pulled the material low enough to allow my cock to spring up, tucking the elastic under my balls to add to the exquisite torture. He took my length in his fist and stroked. "Looking forward to earning enough points in the ultimate package to cash in and move to playing with that gorgeous ass of yours." He licked my tip. "Love this." To prove his point, he swirled his tongue around and sucked my head briefly. "But want that ass too," he growled. "Not gonna lie, wouldn't mind this pretty cock in my hole either." His words were hot against my throbbing flesh.

I threw my head back and moaned. "You switch?" When he nodded, I whimpered. "Good to know." *So very good*. "Now suck me," I demanded.

Danny smiled and never took his eyes from mine as his mouth engulfed my dick. He gripped my hips, bobbed his head up and down, and took me deep while I thrust and moaned. When his hands cupped and teased my balls, I couldn't stop the release that roared through me.

I watched as Danny swallowed everything I gave him, licked me clean, wiped his mouth with the back of his hand, and smiled mischievously as he popped the button on his jeans with a cocked brow.

Licking my lips, I nodded greedily and reached for him as he pulled his pants and boxer briefs off to reveal a long, thick cock ready and waiting for my mouth. "I want it rough," I said as I grabbed his ass and pulled him forward to straddle me. By this point, I was nearly flat on the couch. His legs around my torso and chest put his cock right at my mouth. "Want it so deep and hard I gag and get tears down my cheeks."

"Don't want to hurt you," Danny whispered as he ran a hand through my hair.

"You won't. I'll stop you if it's too much. Don't always need it that way, but I love it. Want you to use me, fuck my face, take me hard." I flicked my tongue out and tasted his precum.

Danny groaned and fisted his cock before smearing the pearly liquid on my lips. "Open for me," he demanded.

I obeyed and he fed me his cock, inch-by-inch, until his balls met my chin. I caught his eyes, my nostrils flaring as I breathed around his invasion, and nodded my head in hopes that he'd give me what I wanted.

He grunted, shifted slightly, and gripped the back of the couch as he began to fuck my face exactly the way I wanted it. He thrust deep causing me to gag and I loved it. I ran my hands over his firm ass and teased along his crack. Even just imagining him bending over for me was enough to have my dick interested again.

"Gonna come," Danny warned as he continued to pound my face. He thrust deep and unloaded thick, hot, salty spurts into my greedy mouth. When his spent dick slipped from my mouth, Danny gathered me close and collapsed our bodies in an awkward heap on the couch.

After rearranging our limbs, he cupped my face and looked at me very seriously. "Are you okay? Was that too much?"

I kissed him, moaning into his mouth as our flavors mixed on our tongues. "That was fucking amazing. Exactly what I needed. I loved it."

"Just don't ever want to hurt you," he murmured against my mouth.

"You didn't. Was it good for you?" I bit my lip. "It seemed like you enjoyed it. Was I okay? Sorry I came so soon, it's been a while and your mouth is fucking amazing, and…"

He kissed me, thrusting his tongue deep. "So, a tongue

or a dick shoved in there are the two ways to keep you from word explosions. Gotcha."

We laughed, lips and teeth bumping, and I realized it had been a very long time since I felt as comfortable, content, welcome, and wanted as I did right then. "I'm really glad I met you," I whispered. Before that statement could seem too serious, I joked, "No one else I'd rather share the ultimate package with."

Danny's eyes twinkled and he smiled. "I'm really glad I met you. Not sure my jaw muscles can handle all the smiling, but I'm really enjoying the ultimate package. So glad I upgraded." He winked.

"Oh, so smiling is the only thing causing your jaw muscles problems? I need to up my game." I kissed him again.

When our dicks made a valiant effort to prepare for round three, we both laughed and rolled from the couch. Once our clothes were back in place, we spent several moments just holding each other and kissing.

"I like this about you," I mumbled against his chest.

"What?"

"That we can go from rubbing off to eating bar food to sucking each other like Hoover vacuums to just cuddling all in one evening. Doesn't feel weird or forced or too much. It just feels like *Gabe* and *Danny*, like *us*, and I like it." In truth, I liked it *a lot* more than I should have. Warning bells were going off in my head. Don't get too attached. You guys are friends, don't go falling in love.

My heart hitched in my chest and I pushed away the sneaking suspicion that it may have been too late.

4

DANNY

Gabe and I spent the next day apart.

I kinda hated it, but I knew it was for the best so we weren't smothering each other. We texted a lot. He got his laundry done, binged some shows, and took a nap to prepare for his next stretch of shifts.

I took a few appointments, worked on my own bike, dreamed of warmer weather so I could go for a ride and not freeze my ass off, and read the book I'd picked up at Indy Reads Books when Gabe and I went shopping.

I rolled my eyes and laughed as I thought of Gabe's reaction when I said I liked books.

"You really like to read?" Gabe had screwed up his face. "I mean, it's a good hobby, just doesn't hold my interest for very long."

While he was working his three twelves later that week, I kept busy at work. But texting with him throughout the day quickly became a favorite. We talked about completely random shit, but it never failed to make me smile.

I told him about cutting myself on a chain, finding a dead mouse in a rebuild, and how Bay kept trying to get me to go see Kyson for a massage.

Gabe told me about three sets of shots he had to give, a kid throwing up on the doctor, and getting peed on by a baby.

On the day we were going to hang, I checked the clock on the wall of the shop and tried to stay busy waiting for Gabe to come downstairs. Every creak and step made me stop and glance up. I was pathetic.

Just as Gabe came bounding down the steps, a harried-looking Bay came into the garage with a smiling, babbling Cori on his hip. The adults said hello, the baby just waved and gurgled. Then Bay glanced between Gabe and I and winced.

"What's up, boss?" I wasn't sure I'd ever seen Bay look anything but calm, cool, and collected.

"Um, I've got a huge favor to ask." He shifted Cori and the diaper bag. "I have to go get Arlo from school for an appointment. Kyson was supposed to come get Cori from me here at the shop, but he's running about twenty minutes late. I can't wait twenty minutes or Arlo will be late for the appointment."

While I had heart palpitations over what Bay may be leading up to, Gabe stepped forward with a huge smile.

"We've got her." He reached his hands out for Cori. The baby smiled and grabbed for him with a slobbery hand. "Go on. Leave her bag. Let Kyson know she's here. We'll go upstairs and play for a while."

Bay shot a look at me and then back to Gabe. "Are you sure? I'm so sorry to ask. I've never left her with anyone but family," he rambled. "Shit," he winced, "shoot, you *are* family. And you're a nurse. A pediatric nurse. You know kids and life-saving procedures. Okay, thank you guys so much. Seriously, so much." Bay gave Cori a kiss, shoved the bag in my arms, and rushed off.

"Don't look like he just left us with a poisonous snake. She's a baby. It's twenty minutes. Thirty at most." Gabe hip-checked me. "We've got this. Come on, let's go upstairs."

"What are we going to do with her?" I asked, horrified at being left alone with a baby.

"We'll see what toys she's got in her bag, maybe a snack, talk to her, and entertain her for a bit. Kyson will be here before we know it." Gabe pushed open his door and jostled the little girl on his hip. "Right, Cori? We'll be besties until Daddy gets here."

He sat on the couch and balanced her on his lap. "Bring that bag over here. Let's see what we've got."

"What if she pees or something?" I whispered as I sat beside him.

Gabe laughed. "This is a diaper bag, it likely has all we'd need for that. As long as it's not *on* me, I'm good. And even then, I can handle it." He rummaged through the bag and pulled out a couple toys. Cori wiggled on his knee and he put her down. Once the little girl had steadied herself, she grabbed a colorful toy and stuck it right in her mouth. "That's the biggest thing with her being here. My apartment isn't baby-proof so we have to keep a close eye on her."

Cori reached into the bag and pulled out a soft-cover book, toddled over to me, and held her hands up.

I shot a look toward Gabe and shook my head. "What's she doing?"

He smiled and laughed. "She wants you to read her book. Pick her up. You've held her before, I saw you at Christmas."

My cheeks heated, mostly from terror, as I reached down and hefted the baby to my lap. She was heavier and seemed sturdier than I expected. Babies always seemed like they'd break if I touched them. Cori shoved the book in my hands and yanked the cover open.

"Wed," she exclaimed and clapped.

I glanced at the page. Sure enough, it was a page of all red.

"Read the words and point to the pictures," Gabe murmured as he leaned against my shoulder.

I cleared my throat. "Red." I pointed at the word. "Red ball."

"Ball!"

I smiled. "Red fish. Red circle. Red strawberry."

Cori reached for the book and turned to the next one. "Bue!"

"Blue." I pointed at the word. "Blue bird."

"Biwd!"

"Blue square. Blue butterfly. Blueberry." I finished the page and let Cori turn it again.

"Geen," Cori stated and pointed.

"Is she reading this?" I asked quietly.

"Not exactly. She's probably recognizing a lot of the colors and she's likely heard it enough to know which pictures and words go with each color," Gabe explained. "It's the beginning stages of reading and very important. Kyson and Bay are doing an amazing job with her."

"Geen!" Cori demanded.

Properly reprimanded, I went back to reading. "Green. Green grass. Green triangle. Green apple."

Cori helped turn the pages, announced the colors, and clapped for each page after I read it. When there were no pages left to read, Cori did something with her hands and said something that sounded very much like, "All done."

"Ohhh, I think that's the sign for *all done*. It's sign language for babies. We've got babies at the office who know a few signs—up to thirty or more. *More*, *again*, *milk*, *eat*, words like that are important to teach little ones. It helps them communicate." Gabe took the book and pulled out a plastic can that reminded me of Pringles, but smaller.

"That's so cool," I remarked about the sign language, but pointed at the item he held. "Chips?" I wasn't sure Bay and Kyson were the type to stuff their kid with junk food.

"No." Gabe smiled and shook the can. "They're veggie puffs." He took the lid off and Cori toddled toward him.

Cori gestured with a hand at her mouth, like she was putting food in. "Eat."

"Did you see that? It's the sign for eat." Gabe beamed at her. "You want a snack?"

Cori plunged her hand in the puffs.

"Here," Gabe said, "let's do it this way." He poured some puffs in his hand and held them out to her.

The little girl grinned, picked up a puff, popped it in her mouth, and made a big show of saying *Mmmmmm* before doing it all over again. As she was putting the last puff in her mouth, a knock sounded at the door.

As ridiculous as it sounded, I kinda didn't want to stop

watching Gabe with Cori, but I stood and went to let Kyson in.

"Oh my gosh, thank you guys so much for watching her," Kyson said as he rushed in.

We both paused and watched Gabe and Cori play peek-a-boo for a moment.

Gabe played it up and pretended to gasp. "Oh look, Cori. Who's here?" He pointed toward Kyson.

"Dadda," Cori exclaimed and clapped. She made the sign for eat. "Eat."

"I know, baby girl. You're hungry. I'm sorry for being late." Kyson knelt down and hugged her close. "Did you have fun with Danny and Gabe?"

"Book," Cori babbled and made a sign that looked like opening a book. Then she patted my leg and giggled.

I blushed and cleared my throat. "We read her color book. It was almost like she knew the words." I couldn't help the smile on my face as Cori continued to pat my leg. "She's amazing with that baby signing," I stated. "I wouldn't have known what she was doing, at least not right away, but Gabe recognized it. So cool."

"It's been a lifesaver. She picked up on it much quicker than she picked up on verbalizing words, so it gave her a way to communicate and kept all of us from going insane." Kyson picked his daughter up. "She loves that book. We probably read it about twenty times a day."

Gabe packed Cori's bag. "If you ever need help in a pinch, we're always willing to watch her." He bit his lip and wrinkled his nose. "Well, *I'm* always willing to watch her and Danny will get used to it."

I shrugged. "I didn't break her, so I'm counting it as a win."

"Be careful of your offers, we only trust the kids with a few people. Seeing you guys with her just now, and knowing you're a registered pediatric nurse, you just soared to the top of the list." Kyson winked and took the diaper bag. "Hey, we didn't end up having a big New Year's Eve party because Ginny was feeling bad, the kids both had ear infections, and Rhys had a sinus infection. *But* we're planning a party to make up for that. You guys should come." He glanced toward Gabe. "The guys and I want to get to know you. I've only ever had those two knuckleheads for cousins, I'm happy to add you to the circle."

Gabe's eyes grew wide. "Wow, that would be great. Thanks. Can you let me know the date and time? I'll try to make it work."

"Sure thing. I'll get your number from Bay." He hefted the bag on his shoulder and shifted Cori. "I've gotta get her some lunch before she becomes a banshee, but thanks again for your help. You both should think about coming by for a massage." He grinned. "Can even make it a couple's massage if you'd be interested."

My face caught fire, but Gabe just laughed.

When Kyson was gone, I wanted to ask why Gabe didn't accept the invite right away, but I figured he had a reason and maybe needed a little time to think it through.

"You're amazing with kids," I said as I kissed his cheek. I knew we had plans to eat lunch and possibly meet up with Chase and Xan a little later, but we weren't in any hurry.

"She's adorable and easy-going. There are some kids in the office who make me want to pull my hair out." Gabe frowned. "Actually, it's more the parents' lack of discipline that drives me insane. Some parents are so great. Some are so *not*. The ones who act as if their kids are perfect angels or the ones who want to be their kid's best friend and *never* tell them no are the ones that drive me insane the most."

"Do you have certain patients you always see?" I asked.

"Depends. A lot of times we see the same patients for well-child appointments, but we often get others assigned to us if it's a sick visit or a certain date or time was needed." He walked to the couch and sat down.

When I joined him, he stretched out and put his feet on my lap.

"Do you have favorite patients?" I rubbed his foot and tried not to get turned on by the way he moaned and leaned his head back on the couch.

Gabe smiled. "I'll never admit it, so don't try to get me in trouble. Most of the babies are adorable and I love seeing them. The bigger kids, like tweens and teens take a special approach. I like all kids, but probably nine months to two years are my absolute favorite." He wiggled the toes of his other foot and I moved my rubbing. "Some of the nurses have been there since the doctors opened the practice and have seen babies grow up and now they see them at their teen year appointments. That's crazy to me. I think of these little tiny babies and how there's no way they'll one day be teenagers. Even crazier is thinking of how old I'll be by then."

"What? Like 41?" I snorted. "Ancient."

"That's not *that* old, I know. It's just weird to think of babies growing up and me just giving them medicine and shots and checkups year after year until they're nearly adults themselves." His head lolled against the couch.

"So, who are your favorites?" I dug my thumb into the sole of his foot.

"I don't like to pick favorites, but there are about five I'd say I'm especially fond of. There's this set of twin boys, Hayden and Ian. They are so fucking cute. They are about one year old and they talk and laugh and are just so adorable. Then there's this little boy, his name is Terrell. He's got the biggest brown eyes, these eyelashes that are like a mile long, and a smile that lights up a room. There's a new baby who had a lot of trouble when she was born, but she's getting so much healthier and it's great to see her come in every month." He smiled and the love he had for his patients was evident. "But my overall favorite is probably Eden. She's three, huge blue eyes like her mom, but dark skin like her dad, gorgeous ringlet curls. She's got the cutest little voice. Her mom is pregnant and Eden is so excited about the new baby. She's a good kid. Polite, curious, funny. Loves to read, loves preschool, likes to catch bugs. So damn cute. And her parents are great. They're fabulous with her. Come to all her appointments together—that may change with a new baby—" he laughed, "but they just seem like really good people all around."

"I don't know that I've ever even known the name of more than maybe three kids in my life. The fact that you're around so many on an almost daily basis just blows my mind," I mumbled.

"Speaking of blowing your mind," Gabe teased and rubbed his foot against my crotch.

"No, we're going to lunch. Xan said something about

an arcade with good drinks. Or we could go to a movie." I stood and pulled him to his feet. "You can blow me *and* my mind later."

Gabe laughed and snuggled against me.

I'd never been a touchy-feely person, but with Gabe, I realized it wasn't because I didn't like it, it was because it had never been offered to me. He was such a cuddler, and I quickly learned to love it and missed it when he wasn't around.

"You want to talk about that invite?" I murmured against the top of his head.

He tensed. "I don't know. I kinda froze."

"Tell me about it as we head to lunch." I glanced toward the window. "No snow or rain, want to walk or drive?"

"Let's just walk, it's not terribly cold," Gabe said.

Once we were down the back steps, we headed down the street.

"Where we eating?" I asked.

"BRU Burger?" Gabe suggested.

"Perfect." Their burgers were amazing. "Now, tell me about that invite."

He took a deep breath and blew it out of puffed cheeks. "So, I've known about my father and brothers—and Kyson—for about two years. At first, I was determined to find my father and his kids. Then I found him and met him and realized I wanted nothing to do with him. That sent me spiraling backwards a bit wondering if his sons were anything like him. But my curiosity got the best of me and I continued looking until I found them." Gabe's words were pouring out and I wanted to hold him, but I just let him talk as we walked.

"I was shocked and relieved when I found them and realized they were gay like me. Honestly, I cried. It meant that Dick didn't just hate me, he was probably the same toward them. I didn't like that he was that way, but at least I wasn't alone—I'd been alone most of my life, with the exception of my mom—and I couldn't handle Dick and my brothers all hating me. Once I found them, I was hit with an *oh shit* type moment of *now what*? 'Hey guys, I'm your illegitimate brother and I've been stalking you. Can we hang out sometime?' Then Bay had the apartment and there was no way around it, I *had* to let them know who I was. I couldn't keep that secret." He pulled his hood up and shoved his hands in his pockets. "They *accepted* me. They were fine with me living there. They basically took my side against Dick almost immediately. They all seem like great men and they've done nothing to make me feel unwelcome—even if we don't know each other well yet. And an invite to a party to hang with them and get to know them and their chosen family is all I've ever wanted." He stopped talking and glanced my way.

"But?" I encouraged.

Gabe smiled softly. "I love that you get me so easily." He nudged his elbow against my arm. "I'm having a crisis of the mind. I don't want to go and be the odd guy out or third wheel. What if they don't like me? What if we have nothing in common? What if they decide Dick was right and I'm a huge waste?"

"Hold that thought," I mumbled as I opened the door to BRU Burger.

A few moments later, seated and drinks ordered, I gestured toward his menu. "Once we have our orders decided, we're going to continue that conversation."

Gabe nodded and looked over the options.

When the server brought our drinks and took our orders, I slid my knee alongside Gabe's under the table. "First, I'll go with you. If that would help." I wasn't sure how having me with him would *help*, but I was willing to do it if it made things better for him.

A smile filled his face and his eyes got suspiciously bright. "Are you sure? I know parties aren't your scene."

"They aren't. But I know the Silvers and most of their extended group. I know it's important to you, so if you need me there, I'll be there."

Gabe swallowed and nodded. "Thank you. That means a lot."

I shrugged. "It's what friends do." I winked and nudged his knee. "Now, regarding all the worries you have. I think it's normal; I get the fears. But there's no way they won't like you. They are pretty much estranged from their father anyway, so they definitely won't take his side over yours. And if for some reason they do, you've got me. Not a great consolation prize, but I'm here."

He wiped at his eye and laughed. "I love you."

I froze and waited for him to correct himself.

But all he did was shake his head and smile. "Like for real. Friendship love. Maybe even bigger love—and I'm sorry if that's scary, but you get me, you make me better, you brighten my days, and sex or no sex, I love you."

My heart beat hard in my chest and I fought the urge to drag him to a dark corner where I could hold him close and kiss him. Were we doing this? Was I ready for this? Without another thought, I dove in headfirst. "I totally get that. It *is* scary as fuck because I figure I'll either fuck it up or you'll come to your senses soon, but I love you the same way. How it got to this point—hell, *when* it got to this point—I don't know, but I know that my life is better with you in it. *I'm* better because of you. I never knew how alone and down I was until you shone light onto my life. If we stopped whatever sex we're doing right this second, I'd still love you and be happy to have you as a friend."

Gabe pulled a face of mock horror. "But we're not going to stop that, right? I was pretty much kidding about all of that *sex or no sex* part. Because I was really looking forward to the sex part of our friendship."

I laughed. "Pretty sure this is a lot more than a friendship by this point. I would have scoffed at anyone else who took the path we took, but nothing about this seems too fast or rushed or unnatural to me. I'm looking forward to continuing what we're doing for as long as we are both on the same page."

"Does that page include butt stuff?" Gabe whispered.

I nearly choked on my water and glanced around quickly to make sure no one had heard him. "Oh my God, yes. But you don't have to say it aloud out in public."

Gabe grinned. "My bad," he teased. "It's so weird how quickly our friendship took root and grew into something so amazing. I'll take credit for that since there's no way you would have approached me to be friends."

I smirked. "True. But there's a strong pull between us, I may have had no control over it even if I'd tried to fight it."

His knuckles brushed against mine. "Resistance is futile, don't try to fight it."

"Don't even want to," I murmured.

As our food was placed before us, I fought against the

unfamiliar feelings of happiness, contentment, and being wanted—*needed*—and my heart was tugged in several different directions all at once. These were new feelings. I used to be able to bury things, convince myself I didn't need or want anything more, but now I had another heart to be concerned about. My heart? Yeah, I'd prefer it not be busted up. But Gabe's heart? I wanted to love it—love him —and protect both with everything I had. *Holy shit*. The words, the feelings, the excitement, the fear, it was all damn overwhelming.

But when Gabe hooked his pinky finger with mine before smiling and popping a fry into his mouth, I couldn't help but feel like damned Superman—ready and willing to take it all on.

As we left BRU Burger, Gabe turned to me. "So, that was a lot back there. It feels like we decided something big, but I don't want to think it was big and have you not feeling the same. You'll go with me to the party, right? But I kinda totally threw out love and I totally mean it, but I can see how it might have been too much and I didn't expect you to say it back so don't feel like you have to stick to that or anything. It's kinda freakin' me out so it's *got* to be freakin' you out…"

Not being one to shove my tongue down his throat on the street, I put my arm around him and my hand over his mouth. "Shut up," I teased and bumped my hip against his.

Gabe laughed and nodded.

"Our entire friendship has been *a lot* from day one, but I've never once regretted it or wanted it to be different. As long as you'll have me—and as long as what we have seems good for both of us—I'm completely on board with what we're doing, the speed we're doing it, and I *do* love you. It's a definite combo of a platonic love and a romantic love. I'm pretty sure I've never *loved* anyone before—I guess I loved my parents, but that was a *long* time ago and we weren't even super close—so it's overwhelming, but the feeling isn't bad. Hell, you've got me going out, having fun, and speaking in entire paragraphs. Pretty sure I can say that whatever we're doing is good for me and I'm all-in."

I yelped and jerked away when Gabe licked my hand.

He laughed and I wiped my hand on my jeans as we moved to the side to let a couple walk past us.

"Holy shit," a voice exclaimed. "Murder? Is that you?"

I froze and my entire body went cold.

Gabe's muffled noise was a mix between a gasp and a growl when he heard the old nickname. He'd sworn to never call me that and he often corrected the guys at the shop if they called me Murder—even they never meant any harm by it.

The moment I turned my gaze toward the speaker, I knew exactly who it was.

Joe Unger. Talk about a blast from the past. And not a welcome one.

"It's Danny," Gabe challenged.

Joe's eyes went wide, his dark caterpillar-like brows climbing high. "Yappy little guard dog ya got there, Murder," he sneered. After an up and down of Gabe, Joe spoke to me. "Haven't seen you in ages. You been hiding up here in the big city?" He glanced between Gabe and me. "Who would have thought that *Murder* Murdoch would run to the city and get himself a piece of fairy ass?"

I clenched my fist and took a step toward Joe, but Gabe angled himself so he was slightly blocking my advance.

The woman next to Joe made a grumbly remark and he rolled his eyes. "Yeah, go on. I'll be there in a bit. No purchases until I approve," he threatened and slapped her ass as she walked away. She kept her eyes down as she scurried off.

"My wife wanted to visit the city and see some craft stores. It's our anniversary; been putting up with her damn craft shit for well over ten years, guess I can let her get some yarn and eat at a fancy restaurant." Joe winked and offered a smarmy grin. "When you've got the money, may as well spoil her."

I crossed my arms over my chest, swallowed my fury, and absorbed Gabe's heat as he leaned into me.

"I'm a car salesman down in Martinsville. One of the biggest." Joe nodded.

"I bet," Gabe drawled. "Should be *so* proud." His words were laced in venomous sarcasm.

Joe glared at Gabe.

I bit back a smile. "Good for you." I started to move away and Gabe followed, both of us ready to escape.

"Wait, we should catch up. What are you doing these days?" Joe grinned evilly. "Guess I already know *who* you're doing." He laughed at his own ridiculous joke.

Refusing to let Joe shame me, I stepped into his space and let my icy glaze reign down on him. "I'm a motorcycle mechanic. Gabe is my boyfriend and a pediatric nurse. We really can't chat, gotta go."

Before we were out of ear shot, Joe threw out, "A motorcycle mechanic is the best you could manage? Gay and broke in the city? Sad man, sad."

I gritted my teeth and said nothing. Arguing on the street with a man like Joe was pointless and a waste of my time. But I had to force down a reply. Actually, I had to force down the urge to turn around and punch the fucker in the face.

"I'm sorry, that was horrible. Who was that guy?" Gabe asked. "Clearly someone from your past, but he was awful. Oh my God, were all the people from your past like that? I feel like I need a shower after talking to him. And his poor wife. Surely she could have done better. A craft shop and dinner in the city is all she's getting for putting up with his nasty ass?" Gabe slapped a hand over his mouth. "Sorry, I'm rambling," he mumbled through fingers.

I laughed. "It's okay, I get it. Joe Unger was a nasty piece of work in high school and clearly hasn't improved with age. I'm really sorry. I don't often see folks from my past, but most of them are going to be just like Joe. Nasty bigots. I don't want you to have to deal with that." My heart hurt at the way Joe had treated both Gabe and me.

"Hey, that asshole isn't your fault. We could very easily run into someone from my past—hell, we could run into my own *father*—and get the same treatment." Gabe nudged me with his elbow. "I'm just glad we were able to walk away, even though I could tell you wanted to smash your fist in his face."

"Yeah, I most definitely did." I took a deep breath and unclenched my fists.

We ended up at 16-Bit Arcade where we spent a couple of relaxing and refocusing hours drinking, laughing, and playing games with Chase, Xan, Ty, and Vic. The combination of the six of us was definitely an odd one, but we all kinda just clicked. By the time we left, Gabe was a bit tipsy but he was excited to know all six of us would be at the Silvers' party.

* * *

The party was amazing and I adored seeing Gabe get to know his brothers and cousin and their families. I realized quickly that Gabe was a healer like Kyson. He was *not* the strong silent type like Bode. And I saw Gabe as somewhat artsy—like Benji—even though he didn't seem to have an art hobby at the moment. Gabe was a ball of anxiety and worried he'd talk too much, but I could tell from his smile that he was having a great time getting to know them.

It seemed to make it somewhat easier that we'd already been hanging out with Chase, Xan, Vic, and Ty. Gabe and Ty had hit it off right away at the arcade earlier in the week; I chalked it up to their similar ages. Ty's boyfriend, Vic, had told Gabe he'd teach him how to crochet. Chase and Gabe had Ginny to talk about. Xan was friendly to Gabe, but he and I mostly just talked shop.

So, having the entire group together at the party was a boisterous and highly enjoyable affair. The kids were great. None of them were bratty or annoying to be around. They had toys and a play space in the back in Bode and Sage's office, but they enjoyed interacting with the grown-ups too.

I found myself drawn to Cori and nearly hyperventilated when she reached for me from Bay's arms.

"Awww, she likes you," Gabe said and ran a hand up

and down my back. "Stop looking like he just handed you a tarantula. Talk to her."

Swallowing hard and trying to shift her into a more natural position on my arm, I smiled. "Heya, Cori. How's it going?" *Oh my God, I just asked a barely verbal baby how's it going*. Babies were *not* my thing.

But Cori just giggled, babbled something, and patted my cheek.

Her little hand was soft and warm.

So, yeah, maybe I let her poke at my nose and my scruff and wipe a somewhat slobbery finger on my neck as she pointed at my tattoos. But she was so damn cute, and I pretty much stood stock still frozen in one spot, while she wielded absolute power over me.

A couple moments later, Kyson showed up with some of the veggie puffs—much to Cori's delight. She picked one from his hand, shoved it in her mouth, and then picked one up and put it to my lips.

"Eat," she demanded.

What was I supposed to do? Tell a baby I didn't want her offering? So, I opened my mouth and made gobbling noises as I ate the puff.

Gabe smiled at me so huge I thought his face would crack.

Cori laughed until she got the hiccups.

And since it was funny once, we had to do it about twenty more times. I never got tired of it because Cori was absolutely the cutest thing ever and her laugh warmed my heart. Just as special was watching Gabe as he watched Cori and me be silly. If I hadn't already loved him and known he loved me, it would have been apparent in the look on his face at that moment.

Love.

Shit, was I crazy? Were *we* crazy? Was he on the rebound? Was I just desperate?

No, I'd been alone for most of my life and had never fallen for anyone the way I'd fallen for Gabe.

He'd been broken up with his boyfriend for quite a while. He may have been desperate and determined to find and get to know his brothers, but Gabe wasn't the type of guy who *had* to have a boyfriend.

Had things happened *very* quickly between us?

Definitely.

Were we crazy to think we were just going to be friends?

Absolutely.

Was this one of those *when you know it, you know it* type situations?

I thought so, yes.

So, I was done questioning it. I was done worrying. Gabe and I were real, we were solid, and we owed it to ourselves to see what we could make of whatever we had between us.

My only niggling concern was what had happened with Joe on the street. Would we likely ever see Joe again? Probably not. But there were always going to be people like Joe who would try to degrade and belittle what Gabe and I had found with each other. When it was just me, I could ignore it, bury it, or smash my fist into the bigot's nose and work my anger out.

But now that it wasn't *just* me, I worried. Gabe didn't deserve to have to put up with that shit. Honestly, neither of us did. He was right, though. It probably wasn't just people from *my* past. We both had people from our pasts, from our *family* even, who would maybe try to cause problems.

As I handed a starting-to-get-sleepy Cori back to Bay, I wrapped my arm around Gabe and knew in my heart that we were together for the right reasons and I wouldn't let petty reasons like Joe Unger push us apart. Unless Gabe told me he couldn't handle scenes like that happening from time to time, couldn't handle being in a relationship with me, we'd face the issues head-on and spend our time on important things like loving each other.

By the time we left the party later that night, my cheeks hurt from laughing so hard. Between dancing, karaoke, drinks, food, and great stories, I wasn't sure I'd ever had such a good time. Truly, by the end of the night, Bode, Benji, Kyson, and Gabe seemed like they'd known each other their whole lives. Gabe fit right in and the other guys welcomed him with open arms. I'm pretty sure we'd agreed to a weekend on their farm sometime in the spring—and I loved that Bode promised it would be a weekend when the Porn Brothers weren't there. I couldn't help but laugh at the guys calling their fathers the Porn Brothers, but they weren't wrong. Dick and Rod Silver really did sound like perfect adult film names. Benji had added that we could hit the farm when their mothers weren't there as well, if that was something that would make it easier for Gabe.

Gabe surprised me by saying he held no ill-will toward Bode and Benji's mother—although, I'm not sure *why* he would have—and that if she was okay with him being there, he was okay with her being there.

"You wanna go to your place or mine?" I asked when

we reached the point in our walk where we needed to turn or go straight.

Gabe leaned into my side, snuggled under my arm. "Will you do deliciously dirty things to me no matter where we go?"

"Pretty sure that can be arranged," I agreed as I kissed the side of his head and tried my best not to get a boner as we walked.

"Your place this time. Next time, we'll christen my bed."

Our steps were quicker as we headed to my apartment. Once we were upstairs, I wrapped Gabe in my arms and pressed him against the door as I devoured his mouth. Our lips and tongues glided and pressed as the heat between us built.

"Separate showers for prep time, then we're in my bed until we wear ourselves out," I told him.

Gabe groaned. "And once we wear ourselves out, we sleep it off and go again."

"Perfect. Go take a shower. Supplies are in the cabinet, use whatever you need." I kissed him soundly and swatted his ass as he headed to the bathroom.

I spent the next twenty minutes attempting to control my erection, tossed the sheets I'd *just* washed from the washer to the dryer—so they'd be ready when we inevitably ruined the ones on my bed, checked that the condoms and lube were where I'd put them, and grabbed a couple washcloths for clean-up.

As Gabe emerged from the steamy bathroom, skin flushed and damp, a towel around his waist, I wanted to skip my shower and get down to all the deliciously dirty things he wanted. When he smiled and bit his lip as if he *knew* how badly I wanted him, I shook my head.

"You're evil. I'm going to shower. I expect you in my bed when I get done."

"Yes, sir." Gabe tweaked my nipple and palmed his dick as he walked past me.

The last thing I saw before I closed the bathroom door was Gabe throwing a sultry glance to me over his shoulder as he dropped the towel.

With a vision of that amazing ass fueling me, I prepped and took the quickest shower ever—I planned on topping, but I wasn't against bottoming and wanted to be ready no matter what. When I walked from the bathroom, my cock tenting the towel, I nearly swallowed my tongue when I found Gabe on my bed, flat on his back, legs spread, stroking his cock as his desire-filled eyes bore into me.

I dropped my towel and took my hard length in hand.

Gabe whimpered and reached for me.

I took him in my arms and settled between his legs.

We both sighed as our warm skin connected.

"Could spend the rest of my life like this," Gabe whispered and held me close.

Everywhere our bodies met was tingly, hot, and sending shots of pleasure through my blood. He smelled of my soap and shampoo, but on Gabe it was a new scent, uniquely his.

His hands ran up and down my back, caressing my skin, gripping my ass, pulling me closer. "Love touching you. It's like I'm on sensation overload. You're so warm, such a contrast of soft and hard, and you smell so damn good."

I found myself in a haze of pleasure and emotion as I wrapped him tighter, breathed him in, and kissed his neck. No person or thing or situation had ever filled me with such wonder, such awe, such love. "I love you," I whispered.

"Love you, so much," Gabe answered. "Want you, inside me, hard and fast, making me scream."

I groaned and rocked my throbbing cock against his. "Gotta go slow, don't want to hurt you."

"Been using a toy," Gabe argued. "Prep me, but I can take you. Promise." He pressed kisses along my chest and pulsed his hips into mine.

"Show me," I demanded as I reached for the side table drawer to pull out a brand-new dildo.

When Gabe's eyes went wide, I chuckled. "I bought it when I got the condoms and lube. Figured it could be fun to play with."

"Get me ready, then I'll show you how I've been playing to get ready for you." He cupped his balls. "But I'm not coming until I have you deep in my ass."

"Agreed." I kissed him and trailed kisses down his chest, teasing his nipples, dipping my tongue in his navel as he squirmed, pressing hot, open-mouthed kisses against his hip bones. Licking his cock head and savoring the taste of his precum, I sucked him deep. "Roll over," I ordered.

Gabe scrambled to his stomach and pulled his knees up so his gorgeous ass opened for me. "Please, touch me," he begged.

With my hands full of his ass, I pulled his cheeks apart and blew against his hole. I licked my lips in anticipation when Gabe whimpered. "Gonna lick you, tongue you, and fuck into that pretty hole."

He moaned and pressed against me when my tongue made contact with his most sensitive skin.

I teased his pucker, swirling my tongue, licking long swaths from bottom to top, and dipping my tongue in as he writhed beneath me.

"Finger me, wanna feel that stretch," Gabe demanded.

Slicking my finger with spit, I opened him with first one digit then another. I continued to lick his hole as my fingers stretched him. "Can't wait to see my cock sliding in here," I growled.

"Slick that dildo. Gonna fuck myself while you watch and jerk yourself." Gabe rolled to his back.

I pumped a few drops of lube onto Gabe's fingers and he slicked himself while I prepared the dildo.

Handing him the toy, I moved between his legs to watch as he pressed the end against his hole and began to work it into his ass.

"Stroke yourself while you watch," Gabe said.

"If I jerk myself more than a couple times, this will all be over before it even starts," I warned, but I took my thick length in my fist and squeezed.

Gabe whimpered and moaned as he pushed the dildo deeper. His body stretched and opened for the toy and I realized I was jealous of some damned silicone. "Can't do this very long, want you in me. Please." Gabe slid the dildo in and out a couple times before gasping and tossing it to the side. "Fuck me. Need you in me. Please, Danny."

"How do you want it?" I asked, gripping my cock hard as I tried to get control over myself.

Gabe rolled to his front, lifted onto his knees, and spread his ass for me. "Like this, fuck me. Hard."

I grabbed a condom, rolled it on, and slicked myself

with lube. I thumbed more of the liquid into Gabe's ass before lining up my cock with his hole. I pushed in slowly and gently, in awe of how he opened for me, how his body stretched around me, how he quivered under my touch and my invasion.

"Hard and fast. Make me scream, make me come," Gabe demanded.

Knowing we'd have a lot of time for other types of sex, and knowing I was going to blow quickly anyway, I gave in to his request. Gripping Gabe's hips, I held tight and pounded into his ass fast and hard. "Jerk yourself," I told him. "I want you coming with me."

Gabe began to stroke his cock in a quick, hard motion until he tensed and moaned. "Gonna come. Come with me, please," he begged.

As his ass began to clench around me, I gave one final thrust and unloaded, hot and thick, into the condom with a roar.

After pulling from him and disposing of the condom, I gathered Gabe in my arms. "I love you. Was that okay?"

He turned to face me and snuggled against my chest. "Oh my God, it was so good. I love you. I don't always need it hard and fast, but I definitely did tonight. You enjoy bottoming sometimes? I mean, I'm completely down with being a total bottom, but I'm not against topping if it's something you'd like," Gabe babbled.

I captured his mouth and slid my tongue in deep and slow until we were both breathless. "I've never done a lot of bottoming—and what I've done wasn't all that great— but with you, it's like I can't get enough and I want to experience it all." I ran my hand up and down his back. "I loved taking you, being in you, it was amazing. But I'd bottom for you for sure."

We mumbled bits and pieces of more chitchat until the words stopped and we fell into a deep, sated sleep.

I woke in the morning to a hot hand stroking my cock.

"Good morning," I mumbled and fought against the groan as I fucked into Gabe's hand.

"It will be an even better morning once the guy I love slides this gorgeous dick deep in my ass and makes me come," Gabe whispered and continued to stroke me.

I had a condom on and my dick lubed within seconds. I positioned myself behind Gabe, lifted his left leg, and pressed against his tight pucker until he opened for me with a long groan.

"Fuck, so good. Love how you stretch me, love the burn," he murmured and thrust his ass back.

"Is it too much, does it hurt?" I was going slow, but I'd stop if he was in pain.

"No, it's just right. Can you stroke me?"

I took his long cock in hand and jerked him in the same slow rhythm as my cock plunging into his ass. "Gonna come for me? Want to feel your hot cum all over my hand."

"Yes," Gabe hissed and thrust harder into my fist. "Wanna feel you pumping your cum in my ass."

When his release tore through him, the pulsating clench of his ass sent me over the edge. With a roar, I poured myself into him as he spilled his hot, thick seed over my fist.

"Fuck," Gabe panted. "I could get used to waking up like *that* every morning."

I chuckled and pulled him close as my spent dick

slipped from his body. "Same. That was amazing." I kissed the side of his head. "Good morning," I whispered.

"Good morning," Gabe mumbled. "Can we sleep, do that again, then maybe go grab breakfast? I'll need to leave fairly early this afternoon to get scrubs washed for my next three shifts."

"Anything you want," I promised.

And that's exactly what we did.

5

GABE

I FORCED myself up the stairs after three days of twelve-hour shifts. The first two days had been normal, but the third day had ripped me to pieces. Chewed me up, spit me out, stomped on me, and I was near breaking.

What I likely needed was to shower and sleep for at least twenty-four hours.

But I knew my head would never be able to shut down. The fear, sadness, and hopelessness would eat at me for hours before exhaustion took over, and then the nightmares would seep in and rob me of rest.

I scoffed at my selfishness. Who was I to worry about lack of sleep when so many others were suffering on a much greater level.

Yeah, sleep would be nice. But what I needed the most, what I wanted more than my next breath, was Danny.

I kicked off my shoes, stripped my scrubs and threw them in the washing machine along with the lingerie bag full of another week's worth of lacy panties, and hit Danny's number on my phone screen.

"Hey, what's up? I figured you'd be showered and dead to the world by now." Danny's words washed over me, filling me with hope and love, and I nearly broke.

"Can you come over?" I whispered.

"You okay? You don't need to sleep?" Worry laced his words.

"I need you. Shitty, shitty day. Can't sleep. Need you," I mumbled through the heavy sadness and exhaustion.

"I'll be right there. Can I bring you anything?"

I could hear him gathering his keys.

"Just you."

When we disconnected, I climbed into the shower. With the water turned up as hot as my skin could stand, I mindlessly lathered my body and hair. Then I stood under the scalding spray as if the cascade could wash away my heartbreak. But nothing could. I was in a living nightmare; the fear, the unknown—actually, the *known* was likely what was scaring me the most—my heart hurt. Did I really even have the right to hurt? Was it even my place? Was I just being selfish thinking of my own heartache instead of what others were facing?

When the water finally cooled, I methodically turned off the shower, dried, and dressed in my softest sweatpants and long-sleeve shirt.

A few moments later, I stood at the kitchen sink staring out the window, but seeing nothing. When a key sounded in the lock, I momentarily froze before remembering Danny and I had exchanged keys for "just in case" moments. Relief flooded through me as hot, angry, heartbroken tears threatened to escape.

I turned to face him as he walked toward me. I knew from the look on his face that I must have looked a wreck.

"Oh my God, what's wrong? What happened?" Danny took me in his arms and held me. My big, strong, silent protector. The man who had found himself alone for so many years because of stupid rumors, hateful bigots, and the belief that he didn't belong—wasn't accepted—Danny hugged me close, ran a hand up and down my back, and just let me cry.

When the tears subsided enough to allow me to speak, I rasped, "Sorry, didn't want to be alone. Needed you."

"Babe, you're scaring me a little bit here. What happened?" His large, work-roughened hands cupped my face.

Bile rose in my throat and tears streamed down my face. "I'll tell you, but then I don't want to talk about it. Not right away. I need you to help me separate from it."

Danny nodded.

"Remember Eden? The little girl I told you about? Three years old, great parents, baby sibling on the way?" I took a deep, shuddering breath.

He nodded again, a frown filling his face.

"She's sick. Like really sick. Leukemia." I shook my head. "No more for now. Make me forget. I know I can't ever forget for real. I know it's not fair of me to want to drive it from my head, to separate from it, when her parents can't. But I need you. Need you to hold me, love me, distract me for a while. I need some perspective, but my head and heart are such a gigantic jumble of emotions and statistics and unfortunate knowledge of what the diagnosis means, I can't compartmentalize it." I burrowed into his chest and let his arms hold me, warm me, protect me.

"Anything. Whatever you need," Danny whispered gruffly against my head.

"Will you fuck me?"

Danny pulled back and lifted my chin, forcing me to look him in the eyes. "I will always do anything and everything to protect you, show you my love, and make things right. Is sex really what you need right now?"

I nodded. "Maybe I'm kidding myself. Maybe nothing will help me box up all the shit in my head right now, but I *need* to escape from all of these terrible thoughts, even if just for a while. Need to feel something other than pain and fear for that little girl and her family. Need to feel you, feel your love, feel your protection."

Danny nodded. "Bed?"

I smiled softly. "Time to christen it." I took his hand and led him to my bed.

He shucked his clothes, tossing them haphazardly to the side before stripping me quickly. "No underwear?" he asked when the waist of my sweats slid over my ass.

"No reason, knew they wouldn't be on for long." I shrugged before leaning in and kissing him, sighing as his tongue dipped into my mouth. "Make me forget, or at least distract me," I begged.

Danny reached for a condom and lube from my bedside drawer, placing both on the mattress, before pressing his thickening dick against my lower abdomen. He dropped to his knees, nuzzled his nose against my trimmed thatch of hair, and sucked my soft cock into his mouth.

I dropped to sit on the bed, my legs spread, Danny's head buried between my thighs, and watched as he brought my dick to life with soft strokes and licks.

He stood then and pushed me to the side, positioning me on my back, spreading my legs. I watched in a pleasure-induced haze as he sucked me deep, fondled my balls, pushed into my ass with a spit-slick finger, and then rimmed me. The sensations were overwhelmingly good, but I was in a trance, just watching, moaning, whimpering as he worked my body and prepared me for his cock.

"You okay? This okay?" Danny asked with a frown, likely worried because I wasn't speaking as much as usual.

"Yes, just fuck me," I begged.

Danny shook his head, moved to nestle his hips between mine, and kissed me. He pulled back when we were both breathing hard. "Gabe, I need you to listen real good here, okay?"

I gave a frustrated nod.

"I've never been in love. Never had a boyfriend, not even a friend with benefits." He nudged my nose with his. "So, I may suck at knowing how to handle this situation. I know you're scared and hurt. I get the wanting to feel something different for a while. And I have no problem being used for that. But I need you to know that this isn't just fucking. I'm not going to go hard and fast so you forget right now. I'm about to bust a nut wanting to get inside you, but I'm going to hold you, kiss you, and make love to you. I need you to understand that. I'm not even completely sure of *why*, but I know it's what we both need right now."

Tears stung my eyes. "Never think that I'm using you, I'm sorry if I made it seem like that. You were the first person I thought of when I found out today, the only person I wanted to tell, the only person I knew could help me work it out. I love you, I need you, but I'm so very sorry if you think I'm using you."

"Didn't mean *used* like that. I'm honored to be the person you turned to, and I'm always on board with being that for you, just like I know I can use you as a sounding board, a shoulder, a comfort. I just need you to know that I can't be hard and rough right now; can't hurt you this way in order to forget the other hurt." Danny kissed me, making love to my mouth, as our cocks rubbed, thrust, and throbbed.

"I want you bare," I whispered. When Danny shivered, I gripped his ass and pulled him closer. "What would you think about that?"

"I'd never put you in any kind of danger. I had a physical when I got back to town. All clear." With fire in his eyes, he cupped my face and continued to rut our leaking dicks together.

"I have to have a complete physical for work, and I get tested between that. Haven't been with anyone since my last two clear test results." I bit my lip, anticipating what it would feel like to take Danny's bare cock in my ass. "I've never gone without a condom."

"Me neither, but I'm good with it. We're monogamous, clear of any infections, and I think we're both level-headed enough—even with our cocks dripping and begging to blow," Danny teased and thrust against me. "So, no condom?"

I nodded. "No condom."

Danny pushed a pillow under me, spread my legs farther apart, and reached for the lube. He slicked his cock and spread the slick liquid against my hole, sliding a finger in and out.

By the time he'd added two more fingers, I'd nearly lost my mind. I gasped when he pulled them out, feeling so empty, but in only seconds he was back, the plump head of his thick cock pressing against my pucker.

As he inched into me, slowly and gently breaching the tight ring of muscle, I panted and pushed against his invasion. The pain was a bit more than when I'd last taken him, less ass play before meant more stretching in the moment. But I welcomed the pain, the burn, and moaned as he gave me the last couple inches. When his balls were flush against me, I breathed deeply, reveling in the fullness. It felt so right. I was complete; we were one. "Move, please. Make me come. Wanna feel you pump your cum into my ass."

Danny growled and shifted so we were chest to chest, my legs wide and wrapped around his waist. I shuddered as his arms snaked under my back and his hands levered on my shoulders. He thrust, agonizingly slowly, grinding his hips into me, his long, thick cock filling me, stretching me while his abdomen rubbed against my dick trapped between us.

"Talk to me," I begged. I had no clue what I needed to hear, or why I needed to hear him, but I longed for his voice.

"Never," Danny gasped the word as he continued to roll and grind himself as deep as possible into me, "never been this good. The sex, your ass, your cock, all so good." He bit my neck and I attempted to pull him completely into my body, I wanted him to crawl under my skin, needed him as close as I could get him.

My balls drew up tight.

"But not just that, you. *You're* so damned amazing.

Those eyes, that smile, the way you can't shut up," he rasped against my ear, biting down on my earlobe before licking away the sting.

An electric tingle traveled down my spine.

"So good, so caring, make me so much better." Danny's thrusts picked up speed. "Love you so damned much, Gabe." His thrusts faltered and he roared as he erupted deep inside me.

The throbbing of his cock, the hot cum filling me, put me over the edge and I shot my thick, sticky release between us.

Breathing hard, making grunting and moaning noises, we stayed wrapped in each other's arms until my hip got a cramp.

"Shit, sorry, but I gotta move. Cramp, ow," I hissed.

I whimpered when Danny pulled out, and nearly cried at the gentleness when he rubbed the charley horse from my hip. Once my leg wasn't screaming, Danny padded to the bathroom and returned with a warm, wet cloth to wipe the mess from my ass and stomach. "You wanna talk now or sleep?"

"You need to go home tomorrow? Work?" My eyes were already drooping.

"Took the day off. I'm all yours." He crawled into the bed, pulled the covers over us, and curled his body around me. "Unless you want to be alone."

"No, want you here. Need to sleep, can talk in the morning."

Pretty sure I ended my sentence with a snore.

* * *

At one point during the night, after midnight but long before sunrise, I rolled on top of Danny, kissing him awake. Spitting on my fingers, I reached behind myself to slick my hole—grateful for the leftover lube and cum. Gripping Danny's hard length, I guided him to my entrance. As I lowered myself onto his cock, panting and whimpering with each additional inch, he grabbed my hips and held me tight.

"Ride me," Danny ordered. In the dim light of the bedroom, I watched as he licked his lips while taking in the sight of my cock swaying between us.

I bit my lip, ran a hand over my chest, teasing my nipples, and took my dick in my other hand and began to stroke myself. Every stroke of my cock brought me closer to exploding. Every time I impaled myself on Danny's cock, we both groaned. I loved the bite of his fingers on my hip bones, the force of his thrusts as he rocked up and into me. "Gonna come," I whispered raggedly.

In one swift move, Danny rocketed his hips up, dumping me to my side. Quickly, he rolled me to my back, slid his cock back into my ass, and pistoned his hips hard and fast. His orgasm overtook him just as my cock erupted in my fist. Danny groaned and thrust deep, spilling himself into my greedy hole.

"Holy shit, babe," Danny mumbled, still trying to catch his breath. "You can wake me up like that anytime."

I laughed and kissed him. "Noted. But it's not even close to time to wake up, so let's go back to sleep."

Once again, Danny cleaned us up—well, as clean as could be expected in the middle of the night. The sheets were definitely on the wash list for the next day. And I curled against him and sighed. "Love you," I murmured.

"Love you," Danny answered, one arm curled around my back, a hand in my hair, his other hand caressing my ass as if it was his most prized possession.

* * *

When I woke the next morning, sunlight streaming through the windows, I knew we'd slept late. But the hard dick against my ass was begging for attention.

I rocked my hips back and smiled at the guttural noise Danny made. "Can a cock chafe from too much sex? Asking for a friend."

I laughed. "You don't have to, but I'm already lubed with your cum. Slide it in," I teased.

"How can I say no to that?" Danny's dick nudged between my ass cheeks.

"Not afraid of chafing?" I taunted even as I hitched my left leg up and reached a hand back to open my ass for him.

Danny fisted his cock and fed it slowly into my waiting hole. Once fully inside, he wrapped an arm around my chest, thrust rapidly into me, and whispered, "Jack yourself. Ruin the sheets to their fullest."

I took my dick in hand and began to stroke.

Within moments, we'd both erupted into our third sticky mess in less than twelve hours.

"My ass has never been so thoroughly used and ridiculously content," I joked.

"And my cock has never had that much friction in such a short amount of time." Danny winced. "I think I may need a rash cream."

We laughed and cuddled together for a moment.

Until I sobered.

Danny must have noticed the change. "Want to strip these sheets? I'll shower and go get breakfast. You can shower while I'm gone."

I nodded and fought back a wave of sadness. Waking up after a leukemia diagnosis was probably like this but a thousand times worse for Eden's parents.

We worked together to pull the sheets from the bed. Danny took a quick shower, yelping at one point, "Ouch! Seriously, I think I may have ass burn on my cock. Can that happen?"

I laughed as I pulled the wet clothes from the washer and threw them into the dryer. After I put the sheets in to wash, I eyed the lingerie bag. I need to lay the lace pieces out to dry, they couldn't be dried in the dryer. I shrugged. I felt a bit indifferent and a bit reckless as I decided I'd hang them up while Danny was gone and if he saw them, he saw them. He loved me. The lace would maybe be a surprise, but I was pretty sure he'd never leave me over a penchant to wear pretty panties from time to time.

"Take a shower, I'll be back with food and caffeine in a few. We'll talk if you want." Danny kissed my cheek and headed out the door.

About forty minutes later, he was back. I was freshly showered. My lace wear was hung to dry all over the bathroom, and the sheets were in the dryer.

"Couch?" Danny asked as he held up take-out bags and a drink carrier.

I nodded and shuffled to the couch with napkins.

We chatted over our breakfast sandwiches and hash browns. I sighed heavily at the first sip of chai latte and smiled when Danny seemed to enjoy his just as much. I loved that we were able to support local businesses on Mass. Ave. and the surrounding areas instead of driving a bit farther for fast food.

"You wanna talk?" Danny asked as he brushed crumbs from his shirt and tossed them into the brown bag.

"Yeah, but I'm not really even sure where to start." I pulled a blanket around my shoulders.

"I'm likely going to suck at this," he warned.

"The fact that you're here and willing to listen means you're already winning at this," I corrected.

His cheeks pinked in a way I loved. "Okay, start with the facts. How did all of this come about?"

"Eden had been in a couple times over the past few weeks. Mostly for a fever that came and went, but also for some joint pain, some bruising, and recently some swollen lymph nodes. Overall, she wasn't feeling terrible, but she definitely wasn't herself. After a couple checkups, the doctor sent her for bloodwork. The results showed acute lymphocytic leukemia. She's starting treatment tomorrow." Tears streamed down my face.

"Want to tell me how you're feeling?" Danny took my hand.

"Honestly, there are so many feelings jumbled up in my head and heart, I don't know that I can." I snorted with no humor. "I talk to kids at the office all the time about not bottling up feelings, sharing how they are feeling about something, and now I'm realizing that sometimes a person just doesn't have the words for that."

"Let's try to unjumble them," Danny said and leaned to the side to grab a notebook from the side table. He slid the pen from the coiled wire and drew lines on the paper to form six boxes. "Give me one feeling. We'll break it all down."

"Scared."

Danny wrote the word.

"Angry."

He put the word in the second box.

"Heartbroken."

The process continued for *helpless*, *selfish*, and *guilty*.

"Okay." Danny tapped the pen against the paper. "Want to start on one of these or want me to pick?"

I shrugged. "Let's go in order." I pointed toward *scared*. "I'm scared for her. Leukemia—*cancer*—it's a damn scary word. She may not know exactly what's going on, but I know her parents are terrified."

Danny nodded and just waited.

I wiped away a tear. "I'm angry. I don't want *any* kid—any person—to have to suffer through cancer. But why Eden? Why a little girl, this perfect, adorable, amazing little girl? She doesn't deserve this. Her parents don't deserve this. That unborn baby doesn't deserve to be born into fear and treatments and illness."

He squeezed my hand. "Definitely doesn't seem fair."

"I'm sad, heartbroken. She'll likely have to stop preschool for a while at least. She'll probably lose her hair —that may be the one that kills me the most—she *loves* her hair and getting it fixed and wearing bows. Their entire normal is now fucked and it makes me feel sad." I wiped my nose on a discarded napkin. "And I feel so helpless. I can't be at her treatments. It's not like we're friends outside of the office and occasional checkups. Hell, she likely won't be in to see us for a while because they'll be dealing with chemo and all that comes with that. Sure,

I can deliver a casserole or some shit like that. But I can't *help*."

"Maybe we can figure out some ways that will make us feel helpful—maybe for them and in the bigger picture," Danny offered. "Why do you feel selfish?"

I shrugged and frowned. "I don't know. Maybe it feels like I'm making this more about me than Eden. *I'm* sad. *I'm* scared. *I'm* angry. What about Eden and her parents? And the guilt comes from that too. Who am I to feel all these things when they are gearing up for the fight of their life—Eden is literally getting ready to fight for her fucking life—and I'm sitting here feeling all sorry for myself because a patient is gravely ill?"

"Stop. You have a right to all of your feelings." His eyes went wide and he cocked his head as if replaying what he'd just said. He ran a hand over his face. "Side note, if you ever need proof of how much I needed you, how much you've changed me, how good you are for me, think back to this conversation. I'm a man who used to have very little to say—or very little I thought anyone would want to hear—and I kept feelings hidden under the surface, only letting my stoic, silent façade show through. And now I'm talking about—validating and even offering advice on—feelings and shit." He took a deep breath and shook his head. "But back to the important part. All of your feelings are okay to have. But I think you're being too hard on yourself with the selfish and guilty. You care about your patients. That's been one hundred percent evident to me since we first met. You having empathy for Eden and her family during this time isn't selfish. I get what you mean, but I don't think it's how you should look at it."

I nodded, not completely believing him. "This is the first patient I've ever had who has been *this* sick. I've had broken bones and bad flu and stitches. But no cancer. The older nurses have seen it all. Cancer, heart issues, extreme mental illness—the list goes on and on; they've lost patients and have heartbreaking stories to tell. But this is my first. It makes me wonder if I am cut out for this. Maybe I'm not made of the right stuff to be a nurse." My stomach rolled with that thought.

"I'm not the person who can tell you the right answer to that. Only you can do that. But I do know you love nursing, right?" Danny asked.

I nodded and swallowed the lump in my throat.

"Can you think of spending your days doing anything else?"

A tear dripped from my chin and I shook my head.

"You are one of the brightest and most compassionate people I've ever known—I know I don't get close to a lot of people...or I didn't until you—but you're an amazing nurse. You have to decide if you stay and continue to help people. My vote is stay because I can't picture you doing anything else and loving it as much."

I closed my eyes and nodded. "You're right. I'd be miserable doing anything else. But I'm miserable now. How do I go back to work, back to treating kids, back to acting as if it's all fine when Eden is going to be getting chemo?"

"One day at a time," Danny suggested.

"Yeah, you're right. And I think compartmentalizing it so that the sadness and fear and helplessness don't overwhelm me is the best I can do, at least for now. I've got other patients who need me, rely on me. I won't give up on them."

"What do you know about the type of cancer she has?" Danny asked.

"It's Acute Lymphocytic Leukemia or ALL. The most common of childhood cancers. It's highly treatable; there's no *good* cancer, but it's got a high remission rate. About ninety-eight percent of children with ALL go into remission within weeks of starting treatment. Of those children, about ninety percent can be cured—*cured* is considered after ten years of remission," I rattled off all the statistics I'd looked up. "So, they're looking at a decade of this. Yeah, they'll hopefully get remission within a few weeks or months—but getting that remission will put a toll on Eden's little body—but then it will be monthly checks, yearly checks. The anxiety and fear will never leave. Every bruise, every fever, every ache will be a cause for wondering if the cancer is back. For ten long years. And I don't know that the worry will ever go away." My eyes filled with tears again. "I can't even picture Eden as a thirteen-year-old, but I won't think of her as anything but in remission and cured. I can't." I blew out a shuddery breath.

We sat quietly for a few moments, just enjoying the closeness and silence before Danny spoke again. I loved that about him, how he'd take time to think and gather his words.

"The shittiest part of this is that a little girl is sick. Her parents are scared and hurting. And there's not a ton we can do." He turned the page to a new sheet of paper. "Let's make some notes on what we *can* do."

At the end of about twenty minutes, we'd come up

with meals, gift cards, donations to the Leukemia and Lymphoma Society, Riley Children's Hospital, and St. Jude's Children's Hospital, maybe offering to babysit if Eden's parents were comfortable with it. I also planned to talk to people at work. Eden's treatment and recovery were going to be a journey, not a sprint, and I needed to be prepared to help in any way I could—and in any way that Eden's parents were comfortable with and would allow.

"Thank you for listening and talking things through with me," I murmured into his chest as I curled up against him. "It's amazing what talking things out with a good listener can do. I feel so much better; it's like thoughts and feelings are automatically falling into their separate spaces so I can continue to function. I'm not sure I could have worked all of that out without your help."

"Before I met you, I would have called anyone a liar if they'd told me I'd be having long conversations—actually saying *multiple* words—and talking *feelings* with my boyfriend. And then you came along," Danny grumbled teasingly as he ran a hand up and down my back.

"And then I came along and improved your life, gave you words, and made everything better," I teased.

"You're not wrong," Danny whispered and tightened his arm around me.

"Nah, you just needed a push."

"I *needed* you," he said gruffly.

We fell asleep for a couple hours and I woke wondering what it would be like to have Danny living with me full time. I knew we both needed our own space, but we spent so much time together already. Would he want to give up his space to move to my place? Would he be interested in me moving in with him?

Or maybe I should just stop my mind from running full-steam ahead and let things happen as they were meant to be.

Danny shifted and groaned a waking-up noise. "Gotta piss," he grumbled and pushed at me just enough that he could get up from the couch.

While he was gone, I gathered up our breakfast trash and threw it away in the kitchen. Then I went to the linen closet, pulled out the extra set of sheets, and made the bed. I was putting on the second pillow case when Danny appeared with a strange look on his face.

"What's wrong?" I asked. I really didn't think I could take more bad news.

"Do you have a sister?" Danny asked, but his eyes narrowed as if he already knew the answer.

I shook my head.

"A girlfriend?" He smirked.

I scoffed. "Nope, just an amazing boyfriend who needs to get to the fucking point."

He pulled something from behind his back. "No sister, no girlfriend, but I found *these* hanging in your bathroom?" A pair of white lace panties with light blue bows hung from his finger. "Which leads me to believe that perhaps my hot-as-hell, incredible boyfriend may have a sexy secret he's been keeping from me." Danny swung the undergarment around and around as he advanced toward me like a lion on his prey.

I may have squeaked as I backed away from him. When my knees hit the bed, I squealed and Danny's fiery eyes became even more predatory.

"Are these yours?" he demanded.

I bit my lip and nodded.

"You wear them?"

I nodded again.

"Why?" He moved forward with each word.

"They make me feel sexy and powerful. I like to look pretty," I whispered.

Danny's nostrils flared and a grumble sounded deep in his chest.

"Tell me how you look in them."

His words curled around me and gripped tight.

"The lace is soft and see-through. The back hugs my ass just right and the bottoms of my cheeks peek out," I described breathlessly, expecting Danny to pounce at any moment. I decided I liked tormenting him, so I kicked it up a gear. "My long cock tucks snuggly in the front, but if I get hard, the head sticks out the top. Those are made especially to accommodate a cock and balls, so my testicles are snug, but there's enough room to not be too uncomfortable."

Danny's jaw clenched and he held the lace to his cheek and rubbed it against his skin. "How long have you been wearing lacy underwear?"

I swallowed thickly. "Since college. It's part of why my boyfriend broke up with me. He didn't like it, thought it was too fetish-y." I lifted my chin. "But I like it, like the way I look, like the way it makes me feel." I didn't *think* I had to defend myself to Danny based on the fire in his eyes, but I wasn't going to back down—wasn't going to change myself for anyone. Me wearing lace panties didn't hurt anyone—hell, only a couple people had ever known about it.

Danny had moved close enough I could feel his heat. "Can't keep secrets like this from me, you hear? I may die if I don't see you in these panties. So," he nuzzled his nose against my ear and then ghosted his lips along my cheek to my mouth where he whispered, barely touching his lips to mine, "here's what's going to happen." His hand with the lace went around my back and his other hand gripped my ass. "You're going to bring your two favorite pairs to my place. I'm going home right now to prep myself. You're going to prep yourself here. Then, when you get to my place, you're going to put on whichever pair you want to be wearing when you fuck me —because that's exactly what you're going to be doing. You're going to wear them the entire time and fuck me long and hard."

I nearly choked on my tongue and came in my pants, but I nodded.

"The other pair will be for you to wear while I fuck you," he said.

"I thought you were chafed," I interrupted cheekily and bit my lip to keep from smiling.

"I'll survive." He rocked his hard cock against mine. "You'll wear them the whole time. I don't care how hard and throbbing your cock is, you'll keep the lace on. I want to see your plump head peek from under the waistband. I'm going to enjoy watching that perfect ass, cupped in soft lace, as I push the material to the side, and slide my dick deep inside you. The material will confine your balls while I fuck you, but you'll keep them on. When I pump my hot cum into you, you'll explode and soak the lace with your seed." Danny stopped talking, taking a ragged breath, his nostrils flaring and jaw clenching. "Pick two pairs. Shower and prep. Come straight to my place. We have just over twenty-four hours to play until I have to be at work."

"Fuuuuuck," I whispered and nodded.

Danny cupped a hand behind my head and kissed me, hard and deep. "You on board?"

"Yes, completely." I scowled slightly. "Wasn't sure you'd like the lace, wasn't exactly sure how to bring it up. Thank you for accepting me."

Danny growled and kissed me deeply again. "There is *nothing* I don't accept about you. I didn't realize I had a thing for lace until the exact second I saw these things hanging in your bathroom. Maybe it's just a thing for *you* in lace, but fuck, my damn head and dick both nearly exploded. I love you, always. Kinky, vanilla, lace, cotton, none of it changes that." He kissed down my neck and bit at the soft skin. "But damn, we're going to have so much fun with these."

"And you want the first time I top you to be in lace panties?" I wanted to be sure I'd understood his wishes.

"First time, tenth time, any time. Hell, maybe *I'll* wear some lace while you fuck me in your lace." He kissed me, nibbled at my lip, soothed the sting with his tongue, and shoved the white lace against my chest. "Don't take too long."

I grinned like a damn loon after Danny left. Deep down, I'd known he would accept me, I just wasn't exactly sure what his reaction would be. I guess I'd wondered if he'd be okay with it as long as he didn't have to see it. Or he'd think I was messed up in the head even though he'd never tell me to stop with the lace. But I really hadn't been prepared for such a damn sexy reaction from him. Not that I was complaining. Definitely not complaining.

After a thorough prep and shower, I rummage around for some clothes and threw them in a bag. Since the white lace with baby blue bows were the pair Danny had grabbed, I took those. I also packed the dark pink trimmed in black. My stomach fluttered and my ass clenched as I thought of Danny yanking the pink and black lace aside to expose my hole before he fucked me.

I threw the bag over my shoulder, grabbed my phone and keys, picked up the trash bag to drop at the dumpster out back, and headed to Danny's.

The walk wasn't long, but it gave me time to clear my head and start putting my feelings into sections in my head. I couldn't be down and mopey all the time, even when my heart still hurt. I had an amazing boyfriend—I chuckled, who would have thought Danny and I would become friends let alone boyfriends? I guess my powers of persuasion were undeniable. I had brothers and a cousin I was getting to know—honestly, the time I'd spent with the Silvers had given me hope and a feeling of belonging and family that I'd wondered if I'd ever have after Mom died. They were truly amazing men. I had a job I'd worked my ass off for and, despite the parts that could bring a person down, I loved what I did. Eden and her parents were an inspiration for me. I'd had the honor of knowing them—even just through checkups and the occasional office picnics we held for the families—long enough to know they would face this challenge head-on, with dignity and grace and smiles. Eden was the type of kid who fell down and got up giggling to show you her ouchie. Did she deserve any of this? No. Did I want her to have to prove she and her family could weather any storm? Fuck no. But I knew they could.

It helped to separate my thoughts and give them each a time and place in my head. When I was at work, I focused mostly on work stuff—unless I was on break and smiling like a fool at texts Danny sent me. When I was at home, I focused on home, mostly Danny and my new family. Danny and my family were always there, on my mind and in my heart, but they didn't rule my work life. Eden and her family would always be there, on my mind and in my heart, and I'd give them that space—always—but I wasn't a bad person for letting my life go on. What would happen if every time we were sad or upset about something our entire world stopped? There'd be a huge amount of people unable to live life. I wouldn't do that. In honor of Eden and her fight, I'd keep smiling and moving on.

I still had fear and sadness about Eden, but Danny was a good distraction—okay, he was more than a distraction, but at the moment, a distraction was just what I needed. I hated that Eden and her parents couldn't have a break; they were heading straight into treatment. But I wasn't a close friend or family member who could be there; I knew they had a very large and supportive family. I'd be there for them as their journey progressed. Maybe my most important part would be when Eden went into remission —because she *would* go into remission, I couldn't imagine the scenario in any other way—when she'd come back for check-ups and picnics. I'd be their nurse, their return to normal, their constant when it was all over. And they'd have a baby; I looked forward to having the James family as *mine*. I'd fight tooth and nail to claim them—their family would eventually be my family that I told young nurses about.

I smiled, giving a nod to the hurt in my heart, and knocked on Danny's door. Life was complicated, life was full of ups and downs, but you had to learn to take the good with the bad. I'd be back at work in a few days and fully devoted to Eden James and all my other patients. But in the meantime, I had a bag full of lace panties and a boyfriend awaiting my arrival so a couple rounds of kinky fuckery could begin.

6

DANNY

GRATEFUL FOR A HOODIE TO cover my raging hard-on as I walked home, I pretty much sprinted up the stairs. Once I tore into my bathroom closet and found an enema kit, I forced myself to slow down and do things right before taking a quick shower.

I was an absolute shit show of emotions. For a guy who'd never acknowledged emotions before—hid them, pushed them away, never wanted to feel anything but numb—it had my body buzzing. Sad for Gabe and Eden and the James family. Angry about innocent people getting sick. Overwhelmed and hopeful and beyond happy with what Gabe and I had. Confused, anxious, excited, and disbelieving that I had a boyfriend—that I was seriously, truly in love—when I never in a million years would have thought I'd want that—or even find that. And then Gabe walked into my life.

Like Gabe, I was learning to partition my feelings. It was mostly working. I had a well-paying job that I loved. A boyfriend I was madly in love with and wanted to spend the rest of my life with. *Whoa! The rest of my life?* I thought about that for a moment. Yeah, why not? I wasn't some young kid. I was settled, level-headed, and knew myself well enough to know I'd never want anyone but Gabe. If he'd been a different person—younger, naïve, flighty, *anything* like that—I would have maybe wondered if he could make the decision for us to be *it* for him. But Gabe was a wise soul and intelligent mind in a sexy young body. Growing up without a father, losing his mother, and putting himself through school forced him to grow up and I trusted that he knew what he wanted.

As I climbed out of the shower and began to dry off, I was very much aware of my most pressing feeling at that moment: *lust*.

Finding those lace panties in Gabe's bathroom had boggled my mind. I swear I stood there for a full sixty-seconds trying to sort through what I was seeing and then another whole minute trying to figure out how I felt about it.

It wasn't like I didn't know some men enjoyed wearing silk, lace, leather, lingerie, *whatever*. But I'd never known anyone who wore those items. Or at least I'd never *known* that I knew men who wore those things. What did I think about it? How did I feel about it? I'd pictured Gabe's perfect V dipping under lace, his long cock tucked under the fabric, his ass hugged by the lace, and nearly busted a nut in his bathroom.

I thought it was sexy as hell.

I felt totally turned on.

And I needed to see Gabe wearing lace, needed to feel the material under my hand on his hot skin as I fucked him, needed the rub of lace against my skin as he slid deep inside me.

I'd already taken a day off work, so I *had* to get to the shop the next day. But I had every intention of enjoying the hours Gabe and I had until then.

If he needed me for talking through his feelings over Eden, I'd be there.

If he needed me for talking about his dad or his brothers, I'd be there.

But unless or until he needed me for those things, I planned to keep him in my bed, a cock buried deep in one of our asses, for as long as possible.

* * *

When Gabe knocked on my door, I forced myself to walk instead of run, made my hand open the door slowly instead of yanking it open, smiled and kissed his cheek rather than throwing him over my shoulder and throwing him on my bed.

"Hi," I murmured against his ear while wrapping him in a tight embrace.

"Mmmm, hi. I know I just saw you, but I missed you," Gabe mumbled into my neck.

"You want a drink? Food?"

Gabe shook his head.

"Movie? Talk?" I offered lamely, trying not to Neanderthal the whole scene and drag him to bed.

"I believe we already had plans?" Gabe asked as he pulled away and raised a brow. "Plans involving lots of lace and lube? Pretty sure your sheets will need a good washing by the time I leave."

And with that, all ability to play it cool and calm flew out the window. I gripped the back of his head, pulled gently to expose his neck, and trailed kisses from his Adam's apple to his jaw before capturing his mouth in a deep, wet kiss. "Want you inside me, wearing that lace."

"Just a quick question, for future reference, will I need to wear lace *every* time I fuck you? If so, I'm going to possibly need to invest in more pairs." Gabe smirked as his hands ran over my ass.

"Not every time. Any time *you* want to. Occasionally when *I* want you to. But I can bottom without lace, no worries," I assured him.

"Good to know," he quipped before kissing my neck and biting softly. "But just to be clear, I *really* love this," he palmed my dick, "in my ass. Any time. All the time. For all time."

While he had a teasing tone, his words held something that had my heart racing, my chest tight, and my dick nearly tearing through my lounge pants. "Bedroom," I ordered.

"Bossy," Gabe teased. "You go get in bed. Naked. I need to put on the proper attire. Seems my boyfriend is a kink queen and enjoys lace."

So that's how I, a big, bad biker, found myself stripping naked in ten seconds flat and scrambling onto my bed.

A few minutes later, after I worried I'd explode in my own hand if I had to keep waiting, Gabe appeared at my bedroom door.

Holy.

Fucking.

Shit.

After I swallowed my tongue and squeezed my dick so

tight it hurt, I finally began to breathe again and looked Gabe up and down. From his messy brown hair and blue eyes, to his long, lean legs and somewhat cute feet—I mean, they're feet, how cute can they be? Then I allowed myself to take in his smooth chest and tight pink nipples, his perfect V-lines, navel, and treasure trail, his thick thighs, and finally the white lace panties with light blue bows. I was back to barely breathing. He was breathtaking. The lace sat low on his hips, his balls tight against the fabric, his long cock already erect and protruding from under the waistband. Two tiny blue bows adorned the lace right at his hip bones.

Gabe waggled his brows and bit his lip through a grin. "You like?"

I nodded and motioned for him to turn around.

He obeyed and threw a sultry, teasing glance over his shoulder.

I had to give myself another squeeze to keep from coming. Could a person really come just from seeing a hot dude in fucking sexy-as-hell lace? It appeared I definitely could.

The lace had a seam down the middle that accentuated his ass. The lace ended just above the bottom of his cheeks and cupped the flesh perfectly. I gritted my teeth and moaned, fighting the urge to change my mind and fuck him right then and there.

"Turn over," Gabe demanded as he turned and walked toward me. "I'm in charge now. If you don't like something, tell me. Gonna lick you open, finger you, slide that dildo in a few times, then I'll pull the lace down just enough to free my cock and fuck you."

I shuddered and groaned as I turned to my stomach. I

didn't have a lot of experience bottoming, and what I *had* done hadn't been all that enjoyable, so I was anxious. But I completely trusted Gabe and had no problem surrendering control to him.

He lifted my hips, pulling me to my knees and exposing my hole. The warm breath he blew against my skin made me shiver. When he leaned closer and licked me from bottom to top, I seriously squawked. The next few minutes were a blur of teasing and probing, swirling and licking. I may have lost consciousness a few times. Gabe was a master with his tongue and seemed to find joy in torturing me.

The snap of the lube bottle gave me enough awareness to know he was slicking his fingers. I'd fingered myself for a while in the shower, but it was nothing compared to the delicious sting as he slid his finger inside. He stroked in and out a few times before adding a second finger.

I gasped and he froze.

"No, it's good. So fucking good," I promised.

Gabe continued to work me open. The third finger nearly sent me over the edge. When he grabbed the dildo from the drawer, I'm pretty sure I whimpered. After slicking the silicone, he pressed it against my pucker and began to slowly work it in.

"Fuck," I bit out.

"Too much?"

"No, so good. Feel so full."

"Watching your ass take this is beyond amazing, but I want to see you open for my cock. Are you ready?" Gabe's words were low and breathless.

"God, yes."

He slid the dildo in and out a couple more times before pulling it out and tossing it to the side.

"Look at me," Gabe demanded.

Still on my knees, I looked over my shoulder to see Gabe lowering the lace so that the waistband caught under his balls. "Fuuuuck," I growled.

"On your knees or back?"

Immediately, I rolled to my back. "Want to see you."

"Pull your legs up and open," Gabe ordered as he poured lube on his rock-hard cock. When he glanced up at me, he stroked himself quickly and moaned. "Fuck, that's pretty." He pushed two fingers into me before replacing them with the head of his cock.

The rub of lace against my skin when he was fully inside me took my breath away. "You're so fucking long," I bit out as his cock thrust deeper than anything I'd ever had. The combination of lace, his cock hitting just the right spot, his hot skin against mine, and the tortuous build-up he'd put me through was too much. My release roared through me like a steam engine as I pulsed shot after shot onto my chest and stomach.

Gabe, clearly turned on by the sight, began to thrust harder and faster, the lace sliding against my skin. He pressed forward, bending my legs to an angle I didn't know I was capable of and ground his hips hard. With a long groan, Gabe exploded and spilled his release deep in my ass.

As sensation overload began to ebb, and we regained the ability to breathe normally, Gabe started to chuckle.

"What?" I asked, wincing as he slid out of me.

"That was insanely hot," he answered.

"Yes, yes it was," I agreed.

"And to think, I've got more panties and you promised another round," Gabe teased.

"Give me a couple hours. We'll nap and maybe eat. Then that lace-covered ass is mine," I promised.

* * *

Two hours or so later we'd slept and called The Lizard for food. Gabe asked Sage to deliver at a certain time so we could make use of our predinner moments.

"Dinner is scheduled to be here in an hour." Gabe dug through his bag. "This pair is begging to see some action." He held up a pair of pink and black lace panties. "You game?"

I nodded and stroked my already thickening cock.

Gabe sashayed to the bathroom and I stripped, checked the location of the lube, and studied the bed for a moment thinking about where I wanted him. When Gabe returned, I went back to choking on my tongue and nearly suffocating because I couldn't breathe.

Same gorgeous body, same beautiful smile, now encased in pink and black lace. The majority of the panties were pink, the trim and some ribbons were black. Gabe's cock and balls were snuggly tucked under the material and when he did a complete turn, I was once again taken with how amazing his ass looked in the cheek-hugging lingerie.

"This is going to be hard and fast, just so you know." Gabe moved close, electric heat between us as he trailed a hand over my chest, stomach, waist, ass, and back around to cup my balls. "I don't need much stretching. I want you deep in me, filling me, and I want you to slap my ass through the lace."

"My chafing is grateful," I teased and rocked my cock into his hand.

Gabe froze. "Are you really too chafed? We don't have to. Not at all. I can just wear the lace and jack off on you. I don't want you to be in pain. For real…" he jabbered.

I kissed him, stroking his tongue with mine. "Stop. I was joking. Although, we *will* revisit you jacking off on me while wearing lace." In truth, my dick was a bit sensitive. I'd never had so much sex in my life. But I was hard and ready. No way was I turning down the chance for lacy sex.

"How do you want me?" Gabe purred and bit his lip while shimmying his hips, rocking into me.

"At the edge of the bed, feet on the floor, bend over," I demanded.

Gabe whimpered and went to the edge of the bed, spread his legs, bent over, and glanced over his shoulder. "Like this?" He acted so innocent, but he knew exactly what he was doing.

And the fucker batted his lashes when he realized I'd noticed something about the underwear I'd missed before. There was a slit down the middle. As Gabe spread his legs, the lace gaped open to reveal his pretty pink pucker. "You're going to fucking kill me," I growled.

"Get that gorgeous dick in me before you die," Gabe taunted and wiggled his ass.

I reached for the lube, coated my shaft, and rubbed a slick finger against his hole, pressing in and out for a moment. Despite his protests, I didn't want to hurt him. Pulling the lace apart, I pushed the head of my cock against his opening and slid in gently and slowly, inch by glorious inch. Watching his body open for me, stretch around my thickness, would never get old. When he'd taken all of me, the lace rubbing against my groin, I took hold of his hips. "You okay?"

"Fuck, yes. Move."

I began to thrust, slowly at first, picking up speed and intensity. My hand came down with a loud smack on his lace-covered ass and the whimpering moan Gabe made spurred me on.

"I'm going to come, can't wait. Oh God, so good, so fucking good," Gabe chanted.

As I watched my dick slip between the lace, into his hot, tight hole, over and over, I knew I wasn't going to last any longer than him. I pumped my hips, harder and faster, until my balls drew up so tight they tingled right on the edge of pain, until an orgasm rolled through me and I growled Gabe's name while pumping him full of my cum. My dick pulsed as Gabe's ass clenched around me, milking every last drop from my body. I pulled out slightly, moaning as my cum smeared against the lace, and pushed back in as aftershocks traveled through Gabe's trembling body. "You are so fucking gorgeous," I murmured.

"Fuuuuck," Gabe whispered. "That was so damn good. My ass will *never* get tired of being filled by you."

"Greedy," I teased as I leaned over his back and kissed his neck.

"Accurate." Gabe wiggled. "Dinner will be here soon, then I want a bath. Your tub is nicer than mine. Then we're sleeping. I'll go home in the morning if that's okay."

"It's perfect," I mumbled and realized that the me of the past enjoyed peace and quiet and solitude, but now I welcomed Gabe with me any time I could get it. Maybe I didn't actually *like* the solitude of the past? Maybe I only accepted it because it was all I knew. And now? Now I'd be happy if Gabe never left.

After dinner, we bathed with only cuddles and kisses because our dicks and asses were massively overworked. Gabe talked me into a late-night walk to a local coffee shop for chai lattes. As we walked back to the apartment, Gabe linked his arm with mine and we sipped our drinks while bumping hips and laughing.

"Gabe?" a voice all but squawked.

I stopped walking and Gabe's head jerked to look at the speaker.

"Oh, hi, Jeanie," he answered quickly. "How are you?"

The woman—*Jeanie*—looked as if she'd swallowed a lemon as she looked between Gabe and me. "I'm fine. Um, what's this?" She gestured between us.

I immediately tensed.

Gabe's voice was annoyed. "This is my boyfriend and I out for chai lattes and a walk before bed."

Jeanie's nostrils flared. "Well, I guess you never really know a person." Her pursed lips turned down in a frown. "Does Doctor Renner know about this?"

I was ready to yank him away and tell the woman to fuck herself.

"That I like late night walks and chai lattes? I'm not sure. I'm sure he wouldn't care," Gabe quipped. "Good night." He pulled on my arm and we left a fuming Jeanie on the sidewalk, gaping.

"Who the fuck was that?" I demanded.

Gabe groaned and took a drink. "Ugh, a new office manager at work. She's not been settling in very well because…"

"Because she's a judgmental, homophobic bitch?" I interrupted.

Gabe chuckled. "Well, yes, she does appear to be that. She's just not very welcoming and doesn't get along with the staff as well as others have before her."

"Why did Renner hire her?" I'd been impressed by the stories Gabe had told me of Doctor Renner.

"He was in a bind because the other manager left suddenly due to her mother's illness in another state. He went through a temp agency for a replacement." Gabe sipped his tea. "Renner hasn't been real pleased from what I can tell. He's definitely not planning on keeping her around. But he needs a body while he looks for a permanent replacement."

"You think she'll cause problems?"

He shrugged. "A lot of people at work know I'm gay. Renner knows. Some of my families know. I guess she can try to cause problems, but I don't think it will work." He bumped his hip against mine. "No worries, she's nobody."

Knowing there was nothing I could do but trust him, I finished my drink and tossed it in the trashcan before we headed upstairs.

Once we were home, we brushed our teeth, stripped to our briefs, and settled into bed with nothing to do but chat about anything and everything until we fell asleep. I got the feeling the incident on the sidewalk bothered Gabe more than he was letting on, but I knew better than to push him.

7

GABE

I WAS PISSED. I'd already paced my apartment, slamming anything and everything I could get my hands on. I knew Danny was planning to be done by lunchtime because we were going to eat lunch together since I had a short, extra shift at the office. I didn't want to bother him while he was working, but I was about to explode.

I took a deep cleansing breath and settled in to work on some crochet. Vic Black had taught me some crochet stitches. His boyfriend, Ty, was one of my newest friends and I adored both men. Vic was extremely patient and had spent a couple hours with me one afternoon when I'd popped into The Silver and Gold Creative, the art studio where Vic worked for my brother, Benji, and his husband, Rhys. Danny had been at work, elbow deep in a bike engine, and I'd found myself strolling—okay, Indiana in the winter was freezing, so I wasn't exactly strolling—along Mass. Ave. and stopped in to see the artwork. Vic often had his crochet work displayed and customers could commission him for specific projects. Ty was a hair and makeup guru, but he also did these amazing paper art projects to sell at his uncle's studio. In addition to their work, Benji and Rhys's artwork was on display and was truly breathtaking. My brother was ridiculously talented— as was his partner—and I was oddly proud of him.

Thinking over the morning as I began a chain stitch— Ty was frustrated when I picked up the chain stitch so much quicker than he did when he was learning—I couldn't help the bit of hurt that also seeped in along with my anger. I wanted to talk to Danny, tell him all that had happened. Talking it out would help.

I glanced at the chain stitch and realized it was about a hundred chains long. I chuckled at how caught up in my head I'd been. Counting stitches was not my forte. Focusing on my work for several moments, I began the single crochet stitch Vic had taught me. I only knew single and double for the time being, but Vic said I could make an entire blanket with just those stitches so I was content with practicing my newly-acquired skill for the time being.

An hour later, surprised and pleased at how much the crochet had helped calm me, I tossed the yarn and hook into a tote bag and grabbed a jacket. With my phone, my keys, and my wallet accounted for, I headed down the front stairs to the shop.

Danny glanced up from organizing his tools, grinned broadly at me, looked at the wall clock, and frowned. "How are you already home, showered, and ready?"

I let out a frustrated groan. "It's a stupid long pissy story. I'll tell you as we walk to lunch. The Lizard?"

Danny continued to scowl and eye me like he was attempting to solve a mystery, but he nodded. He knew I liked The Salty Lizard's food, but also that I liked to say hi to Bode and Sage. They were such an opposites-attract kind of pair, but they were perfect together. I likely would have been intimidated by my brother without Sage by his side. Bode could be grumpy and gruff, but Sage mellowed him a lot. Benji and Kyson vouched that Sage's arrival in Bode's life had initially caused even more grumpiness, but once he'd finally given in to the fact that he and Sage were perfect for each other, the sharp edges finally began to soften slightly.

I pulled on my jacket and waited for Danny to finish cleaning his bay, wash his hands, and put on his own jacket. I was already anxious for spring and warmer weather.

"Ready?" he asked.

I nodded.

We said goodbye to Xan and some of the other employees and headed out into the brisk winter air.

"Okay, tell me what's up," Danny demanded. He glanced my way and offered a smile. "Please."

I took a deep breath. "So, I get to the office this morning. I was looking forward to a short shift, talking with others about Eden—one of the nurses is good friends with Eden's grandma—and just trying to get back into a routine even though we're all devasted about the leukemia."

Danny nodded. He pretty much knew all of that because I'd been jabbering about being grateful for the extra shift. But the look on his face told me he knew something was coming.

"So, we're in our morning meeting before appointments start. Doctor Renner had spoken to the James family and was filling us in on her treatment and prognosis—it sounds very promising—and we were going over the day's patients, odds and ends, that type of thing. Very normal." I gritted my teeth and blew out a huffy breath. "And then our dear Jeanie speaks up."

"God fucking damn it, I *knew* she was going to cause problems." Danny's head whipped to me. "Wait, Renner sent you home? What the actual fuck? She got her way?"

I waited for his rant to end. "Can I tell the story?"

He nodded sheepishly.

"Back when we first met, I couldn't get a word out of you and now you're ranting and raving." I bumped my hip against his. "Anyway, she makes this big speech about how she's a professional and she runs an office in a professional way. How she expects to be able to give the very best service to all of our patients. Renner is looking at her like she's fucking crazy. The other nurses are rolling their eyes and not hiding their annoyance. So, she goes on to say that she will *not* work for an office that allows *filth* and *depravity* around the patients."

Danny growled.

"At this point, Renner is pissed. He stands up and basically tells her to shut her mouth. Then she points at me and says 'I saw him.' Her finger was all shaky and her voice was unstable; I expected spittle to fly from her mouth. 'I saw him and his...*boyfriend*, just walking down the street, plain as day, hanging all over each other. Is this the type of office that allows employees and patients, innocent young babies and children, to be exposed to that?' By this point, Renner and the other nurses have moved closer to me and are pretty much surrounding me. If not for her craziness, it was actually a really touching scene. I knew we were a close-knit crew there, but having their support meant a lot."

"So, Jeanie went off the deep end. Why did you get sent home?" Danny was angry. I heard it in his voice and saw the tic of his jaw.

"Renner told me I'd dealt with enough shit for the shift already and gave me the shift off but paid. He started to just kick her out, but decided to go through the temp agency to file an official complaint, report her, and get her removed through the proper procedures. That way she can't come back and say he mistreated her or fired her with no reason."

Danny grumbled, but I could tell he understood that reasoning. "I get it. I don't like that she got to stay, but I appreciate him doing it the right way."

I nodded. "He's a good guy." I shook my phone. "The nurses have been sending me updates. I guess Jeanie is about to have a breakdown, raving about allowing *my kind* to work there. They've given her all the worst jobs— diaper pail duty, cleaning the bathrooms, that type of stuff —to keep her away from the front desk and patients, and also just because she's a bitch and deserves it. Renner plans to dismiss her within the next two hours once it's all cleared with the temp agency."

"So, she'll be gone and your position won't be affected at all?" Danny asked as we walked through the doors at The Lizard.

"Nope, all good. I got paid for five hours but only worked just over an hour. I'll be back for my next three-day stretch. Jeanie has no place with us and hopefully the temp agency drops her ass." I hooked my arm with his.

"Plus, I get to eat lunch and spend the rest of the day with my boyfriend. Definitely all good."

"Perfect," Danny agreed as he kissed the top of my head.

As we headed toward one of the back tables that Sage and Bode usually kept reserved for friends and family—my heart kinda wriggled in my chest. I was *family*—Millie waved us down.

"Just the two men I was hoping to see," she called out as she rushed toward us. For a *very* elderly lady, she got around really well.

"How are you? Ginny said you'd had a bit of a cold?" I asked.

She waved my concern away. "Not to worry, just some sniffles. I went to say hello to my grandson at the shop and he said you two were coming here for lunch. I was hoping I could persuade you to get it to go and take me to visit Ginny." Millie pursed her lips. "I dropped my car with Bay for an oil change and he said it would be several hours." She clucked her tongue. "Now, I don't expect preferential treatment—and I *know* they service motorcycles only—but one would think a grandmother's car could get serviced with a little speed. I think he just tries to keep me from driving." She patted Danny's arm. "Little does he know, I'm a crafty broad and I'll find a way to get where I'm wanting to go."

Danny grinned and looked at me. "I think we could definitely get lunch to go and take you to Ginny's."

It wasn't a question, but I saw it on his face. I loved that he always considered me. He wasn't a pushover, but he cared about my feelings. I nodded with a smile. "Sounds like a perfect way to spend the day." And I was serious. Spending time with Ginny, Millie, *and* Danny? Three truly amazing people and I found myself excited about the visit.

We ordered enough food to feed an army. I chatted with Bode and Sage for a bit while Danny ran back to the shop to get my car—he seemed to know that I wanted some extra time with my brother. Once he was back, we loaded up our order and Millie, and headed toward Rose Gardens.

Ginny had been expecting Millie, but she was overjoyed with her friend, lunch, *and* extra visitors. We spent about thirty minutes eating and talking about goings-on at the facility, what Millie had been up to, and even got Danny to talk a bit about his job. Ginny smiled and gestured toward the door. "I want to hear about Gabe's work, but let's see if the sunroom is open so we can soak up some vitamin D."

Millie grabbed Danny and bustled down to check on the sunroom. Danny came back with a grin and told us to *get your butts down here, the sun is great*—Millie's words obviously—and that's how we found ourselves in the comfy, cozy, sunny sunroom while I told Ginny and Millie about Eden's diagnosis *and* about Jeanie's *scene*. The women were understandably shaken by Eden's situation; they both had little ones in their lives. They were *pissed* about Jeanie.

"I try hard not to wish ill-will toward anyone, but people like *that*—people who hate simply because of ignorance—I have a hard time not wishing karma on that woman. She shouldn't be allowed to work in any location where she can spew her hatred." Millie was seething mad.

"It's all good. I don't like the fact it became an issue—

it could have been a much more sensitive situation if she'd been able to *out* me or get me in trouble the way she planned—she was definitely hoping for a lot more drama for *me* than for her. But she's gone, I got a paid day off, and I was able to see that I've got a lot of great support in friends at work," I explained.

"You're an amazing young man and I respect the way you're looking at things," Millie said. "But I choose to wish her a lifetime of yeast infections."

Danny nearly choked as we all erupted in laughter.

Conversation turned to Ginny's daughter—also Bode and Sage's daughter—Rosie and Oliver, Arlo and Cori, and even Benji and Rhys's dogs Bear and Brawn.

Several moments later, Millie shifted on the small couch. "Oh, I've been feeling so kinky lately."

Three pairs of wide eyes and cocked brows turned her way.

"What?" She rubbed her neck.

"Um, I don't think kinky is the word you want to use there." Ginny chuckled.

"Kinky? You know, stiff, lots of kinks," Millie explained.

"Kinky usually means," I started, knowing my face was bright red, "like unusual sexual desires, maybe like fetishes."

Millie cocked her head and gave some thought to my words. "Ohhhh, I can see how that could confuse some. Like when people say *Netflix and chill* they don't really mean just chilling out and watching Netflix." She nodded. "I learned that from Bay and Kyson. I kept asking them if they wanted to come over for Netflix and chill. Bay would get all flustered and Kyson would laugh. He finally broke it down for me." She leaned forward and whispered, "It actually means sex." She waved her hand away. "If I ever find a man who can keep up with me, I'm going to invite him over for an all-nighter of Netflix and chill—and he better learn quickly that I don't mean a movie on the couch. Lord, you don't even know how hard it is to find good dick these days."

"Oh, but it's so good to find hard dick these days," Ginny quipped and cackled at her own joke.

Between the two women, I'm pretty sure Danny and I nearly popped our eyeballs out of our heads and pissed ourselves laughing. I hoped I was as fun as them when I reached their age.

"Hey, that reminds me of something I started wondering about," I began. "Is there a lot of secret sex going on in here?"

Ginny rolled her eyes. "Secret, not-so-secret, we've got all kinds. There's definitely a lot of friskiness. Pat, old man down the hall from me, he's got a PornHub account and that draws a lot of visitors. I think his grandson pays the monthly fee. But the staff attempts to keep it under control—the porn viewing *and* the friskiness. There are a few long-time couples and they have a double room so if you're unlucky enough—or lucky, I guess, depending on how you look at it—you may hear them getting busy from time to time. Before I moved rooms, the lady I was next to would pull out a vibrator every evening during Wheel of Fortune. Damn that thing was *loud*. But you know, desire doesn't die just because you're old."

"Honey, you let me know if you want a vibrator. I'll get you five of the best kinds. If you've got you someone special in here, or more than one someone special, I can get *accessories* for them as well. Sometimes toys help to enhance things and make it a bit easier. Several years ago, I found this younger man who was very much into older women. He used a cock ring—you know what that is, yes?" She glanced around to be sure we did. "Well, that man could go forever when he wore that thing. I was very much a fan." She laughed. "You know, my faux pas earlier maybe wasn't such a misnomer; I really am a pretty kinky gal." She looked between the little group. "If we were drinking, this would be better, but what kinds of kinks do we have amongst us, I wonder?"

Were my boyfriend and I seriously talking about kinks with two women old enough to be our grandmothers?

"Well, I think we all already know that I enjoy sexual relations with any and all genders—although my precious Rose was the best ever," Ginny said as she spoke fondly of her deceased lover, "and I've done a lot of things in bed. I've always enjoyed a bit of porn from time to time to get the engines roaring if you know what I mean," Ginny said with a teasing grin.

"I didn't discover how great sex could be until I was much older and found a man who knew what he was doing. But I've had a lot of fun learning about toys. I will say, once I spent a few months with a fellow who enjoyed submission and spanking. That was brand new to me; wouldn't need or want it all the time, but it was fun for the time being." Millie raised her brow and cocked her head, waiting for Danny or me to speak.

"Lace," I blurted. All the blood drained from my face and gathered in the fiery tips of my ears.

Danny's head whipped toward me and then he chuckled. Millie and Ginny eyed me curiously.

"I like to wear lace underwear," I mumbled. "And I have *no* idea why I just told you that." I ran a hand over my face.

Danny put a hand on my leg. "It's sexy as hell." He squeezed gently. "Guess *my* kink would be seeing my boyfriend in lace."

"Well now, that's a new one for me, but I'm intrigued," Millie said. "I believe I could find that pretty sexy. *Not* on you," she rushed on, "that would get a little creepy even for a group as close and open-minded as our crew. But I may have to check that out online. It's *amazing* what you can search for on the internet."

"You do you, dear," Ginny reached over and patted my shoulder. "Me, I'm a cotton girl myself, but Rose had a thing for leather and lace—definitely sexy as hell," she agreed with a wink. Then she yawned. "I'm sorry, I think I better head back for a nap. I'm feeling amazing lately, but I still get tired a lot quicker than before the cancer."

My heart clenched. I never really *forgot* that Ginny was fighting cancer—opting out of chemo and treatment meant she didn't have a lot of the same ailments as other patients—but she often looked and came off so great and high-spirited, it was sometimes easy to forget she was sick. "Thanks for the visit. This was a lot of fun. I'll probably be back for a few volunteer shifts in the next week or so."

After we'd gotten Ginny settled in her room, given hugs, and said goodbye, we dropped Millie off with a thanks for inviting us along, and started toward home. But Danny said, "You want to go to Ash & Elm? They've got a new cider of the month. I've not been there, but I hear it's really good."

I smiled. I loved that he was trying new places and wanted me there with him. "That sounds great. You know I love a good cider. I think they have food too, we can do a light dinner since lunch was so huge."

* * *

Ash & Elm was a fantastic little restaurant and cider bar. We sat at a little corner table and each ordered flights of cider to try. After sampling each, I decided on the blackberry and Danny opted for the Fleeting Youth which was a combo of raspberry and lemon. The waitperson also took our order to split ricotta and toast and a bowl of soup.

As we chatted, almost shoulder-to-shoulder, our outer thighs pressed together under the table, I glanced up as a man walked through the opening that connected Ash & Elm to Neidhammer Coffee next door—the two businesses shared the building space.

Fuck.

I must have tensed enough for Danny to notice because he looked first at me and then to the man.

At first, I thought Josh hadn't seen me, but then recognition filled his face and he made his way toward us.

Fuck.

Josh was the *last* person I wanted to see while out on a date—even if it was just cider and a sandwich.

"Gabe, nice to see you," Josh said. He wasn't overly friendly, but at least he wasn't wearing the sneer from the last time I'd seen him—the day I'd come home early and found him fucking his high school football coach. Guess the big beefcake was as far from being like me as Josh could find.

"Josh," I acknowledged.

Danny squeezed my leg.

"Good cider here," Josh attempted idle chit-chat.

"Yeah." I nodded awkwardly. "I hear the crepes and coffee on the other side are good too."

"Oh, yeah. For sure." Josh glanced toward Danny and visibly flinched.

I imagined Danny's face looked exactly like someone who was nicknamed *Murder*. I couldn't help a tiny grin. I kinda loved that Danny would take Josh out in one swing if I even slightly indicated I wanted him to. I wasn't a proponent of violence, and I'd never ask anyone to physically harm another being, but knowing Danny had my back if needed meant the world.

I put my hand on Danny's and nodded my head toward Josh. "This is Josh. Josh, this is my boyfriend, Danny."

Danny gritted out a hello.

Josh's eyes grew wide and he shot looks between Danny and me for several seconds. "Oh, um. Hey, nice to meet you," he mumbled. "Good seeing you, gotta get back," he muttered and threw a thumb over his shoulder. Then he scurried toward the restrooms. A few moments later, we saw him return to the coffee house.

"Who was that prick?" Danny growled.

"*That* was my asshole ex-boyfriend, Josh," I answered and finished my cider. Catching the waitperson's eye, I indicated we both wanted a refill.

"The guy who you caught cheating?" Danny's voice was quiet and deadly.

"Yep. He'd been on me for about a year saying I was

too femme, too gay—he never wanted me around his friends, said I was embarrassing when I was so *out*. He was always telling me I was too clingy and needy—he hated how I always wanted to cuddle. He loved my ass, but it was only for sex. He didn't accept me for who I was, wanted me to change to fit with who he was and who his friends accepted. Finding out about the lace was the last straw. He gave me the option of continuing with the lace and losing him or throw away all the lace if I wanted to keep him." I took a deep, cleansing breath. "I told him I needed time to think about it and went to work. But while I was there, I decided *fuck it*. I wasn't going to change who I was for some asshole, so I left work and headed home to let him know he could fuck off because I wasn't getting rid of the lace. Walked in and found him fucking his old football coach. Big, beefy guy. He seemed to be as gay as they come while he was bent over for Josh, but I'd met the guy out and about and he was the quintessential jock, tough guy who didn't wear lace, ask for cuddles, sound gay, look gay, whatever. Exactly what Josh was looking for." I shrugged. "Josh was an asshole, and he gave in to the pressures of his so-called friends, but I'll never regret getting away from him when I did. I won't change for anyone—I'm me, this is who I am. Too gay? Too *out*? Too femme for liking lace? Fuck him and fuck anyone who has a problem with it." My voice was low enough that only Danny could hear me, but I meant every word.

Danny leaned close, brushed his lips against my ear, and whispered, "I love you exactly the way you are and I would hate if you ever changed a single thing about who you are." He paused. "But I will always support you if you find that who you are changes over time. I know people change; I don't expect either of us will stay exactly the same as we grow and change and discover more about ourselves as individuals and a couple."

The waitperson brought our ciders, took our plates, and left the bill.

"I adore you for saying that, thank you." I squeezed his hand. "To think that when we first met you barely had two words to say to me and now you're promising to love and support me no matter what. I love you for that and I love you for being you." I elbowed him. "But I've *really* got to pee."

Danny chuckled and sipped his cider while I rushed to get the key for the restroom. Of course, just when I needed to piss the worst, there were two fathers with their kids in both restrooms, so I had to wait. I literally was close to doing the potty dance like so many of the little kids at the office, when it was finally my turn. When I returned, I was ready to finish my cider, make a carry-out purchase to stock my fridge at home, and head out.

But Danny was…*off* I guess was the word I was looking for. He seemed distracted.

"Hey, you good?" I nudged him.

He sniffed, shook his head a bit, and nodded. "Yeah, sorry. Cider's got me feeling fuzzy, I guess."

We each bought cider to take home and headed back to the car after paying our bill.

By the time we reached my place—Danny said he'd just walk home instead of me dropping him off—I was tired and ready to shower and lounge around for the rest of the evening. "You want to come up?" I offered.

Danny kissed me gently. "I do, but I need to clean and do some laundry. I need to go home for now."

I nodded. While I would have loved to cuddle with Danny all night, I knew we both had our own responsibilities and lives. It was okay to be apart sometimes.

"We good for lunch after my three days at the office?" I asked, nuzzling my nose against his neck.

"Of course," Danny answered, cupping my chin and lifting my face for soft, sensual kisses. "I'll pick up food and come upstairs. Text me before bed?"

I nodded and kissed him again. "Love you."

"Love you," he whispered.

Danny climbed from the car and I followed. He pulled me into a hug, waited for me to get the apartment door unlocked, and then waved as he headed toward his place.

I showered, cleaned, watched a movie, and settled into bed a couple hours later and never once did the giddy, loved feeling fade. I was pretty sure I had a permanent smile on my face. Sometimes it was hard to believe all the good in my life. I missed my mom. My dad was an asshole. But the good far outweighed the bad, and I felt truly blessed, lucky, whatever a person wanted to call it.

Falling asleep with a smile on my face and dreaming of Danny was something I was getting used to and I never wanted it to stop.

8

DANNY

I NEEDED to walk home in hopes of clearing my head and getting some of the anger out. I'd likely tell Gabe what had happened when he went to the restroom at Ash & Elm, but I needed to process it and stop myself from boiling over before I shared it with him.

I also needed to work out how I was feeling about what Josh had said to me. I loved Gabe more than anything—but maybe loving him meant letting him go so he could find better? My head was pounding, my heart thumping, and my mind reeling with a million thoughts.

In a way, I hadn't been surprised at all when Josh approached the table the moment Gabe was out of sight.

"I knew Gabe had some odd desires and kinks, but I never really pegged him for the type to hook up with someone so far below him." Josh's lip curled as his eyes traveled my body, head-to-toe.

"What Gabe does, what Gabe likes, who Gabe is in a relationship with, none of that is your business anymore. You made it clear he was too much for you, you moved on—in the most

dickish and unoriginal move of all—and so has he." I folded my arms over my chest.

"You don't seem like the type to go for twinks like Gabe. What could you possibly see in him? I promise you, if he hasn't already, he gets super clingy and needy. And he's a complete embarrassment around friends." His eyes narrowed. "Don't even get me started on his kinks."

"You don't seem like the type to be completely stupid, yet here we are," I growled quietly so as not to attract attention. "Gabe is who he is, he's who I fell for, who I love, and it's none of your damn business."

Josh sneered as if I was scum on the bottom of his shoe. "You know he's just playing around, right? He's too high-maintenance to ever be able to settle for you. No offense," he cooed, offense definitely intended, "you don't exactly measure up. Gabe is parties, champagne brunch, and dancing in rainbow cheekies on a Pride float. You're blue-collar, grease under your nails, and beers with the guys. You'd be better off to save you both the trouble and let him move on now." Josh smirked.

"Thanks for the input. You can shove it up your ass. You lost your chance with Gabe. He's my chance now and I don't plan on screwing it up. Now fuck off before he gets back. You're not going to ruin his day any more than you already have." I scowled and clenched my fists.

Josh scoffed, rolled his eyes, and turned on his heel to retreat to the coffeehouse.

I reached my apartment and immediately pulled my free-weights from the side of the living room. When my muscles were screaming, my body covered in sweat, and my arms absolute noodles, I pushed the weights back to the corner and took a shower.

My mind vacillated between anger and worry.

Anger that Josh had thought he had any right to approach me, to tell me anything about Gabe, to indicate that Gabe was just playing or that I wouldn't be able to deal with who Gabe was.

Worry that maybe Josh was right. I was nothing more than a mechanic. I wasn't going anywhere in life. Gabe was this shining star with a bright future ahead of him. Would it be unfair of me to saddle Gabe with mediocrity?

Then I was back to anger at Josh for even putting such ridiculous thoughts in my head. And how dare he indicate that Gabe was anything but perfect? All of the things Josh listed as negatives, as if I'd blanch and be surprised, as if I didn't already know these things about Gabe, *all* of them were things I adored about him. They made up who he was and why I loved him.

Between the walk, the weights, and the shower, I'd finally calmed myself enough to head to bed. I wasn't over it. I didn't have a complete peace about the conversation, but at least I was tired enough to sleep. I had three days to think it over, pour myself into my work, and enjoy texting with Gabe. I wasn't going to let Josh ruin that. He didn't have that type of power over me.

But that didn't stop the lingering, niggling voice at the back of my head from whispering that maybe Gabe would be better off without me.

* * *

I knew Gabe was up when I heard his washing machine start and the vacuum fire to life. He was a creature of habit and his first day off after a three-day shift was always a day for cleaning. I continued working, smiling as

I pictured him moving from room to room to vacuum, dust, clean the bathroom, touch up the kitchen. When my images switched to him bee-bopping around in nothing but a pair of mesh hipsters, I quickly turned up some music and focused on the repair in front of me. Didn't need a damn boner in the work bay.

A couple hours later, my work done and no more cleaning sounds from Gabe's place, I checked my phone.

Gabe: *You almost done with work? We still getting lunch?*

Me: *Yep, if you call it in, I'll go pick it up.*

Thirty minutes later, after washing up at the shop, I pulled open the door to The Salty Lizard and immediately relaxed in the welcoming atmosphere. Bode and Sage had done something spectacular with the place—the food and drinks were amazing, but what really made The Lizard stand out was the atmosphere. Anyone and everyone were welcome—the only requirement was respect and kindness.

I headed to the bar to wait for my carry-out. The place was hopping so I didn't mind that Sage only had a moment to wave and Bode was nowhere to be seen.

"You're the mechanic my son's been shacking up with, right?" a dangerously smooth voice said to my left.

I turned to see a man, glass of whisky in hand, sitting at the bar with narrowed eyes and a smarmy grin.

"Excuse me?" I immediately knew who the man was,

but he didn't need to know that. No wonder Bode wasn't around, he was probably attempting to calm himself in the back before coming out and dealing with his sleaze ball father.

"Oh, come now. No need to play dumb." His eyes raked over me. "Although, I realize it may come easily for you."

I turned on my stool, stood to my full height, and crossed my arms over my chest. "What can I do for you, *Mr*. Silver?"

"Stop seeing my son."

I scoffed. "Fat chance. But can I ask why?"

"He can do better. He's already wasted his education on a damn *nursing* degree. He doesn't need to be strapped down with a mechanic. While I appreciate your vocation, I don't see my son as the type to do the whole blue-collar thing."

"*Your son*," I began through gritted teeth, "is an adult and free to make his own choices. Your son is a damned talented nurse. He's also probably the greatest person I've ever had the privilege of knowing. *You'd* know that if you weren't such a prick. It's bad enough you were never in his life—although, meeting you now that may have been a blessing in disguise—but when he reached out to get to know you, all you gave him was your disappointment and negativity. It's a damn miracle any of your children turned out as wonderful as they did even with them carrying your genes; their mothers must be damned angels. You're a joke. You've got these great kids and you spend all your time sneering and poo-pooing everything they are and everything they do because it doesn't meet your level of satisfaction." I stepped closer and took great satisfaction in the fact that Dick Silver shrank back a bit. "The world is a much better place because none of those boys turned out *anything* like you or your brother."

A very angry Bode plopped my to-go bag on the counter. "Order up."

I handed him my card and waited for my receipt.

"You need to go," Bode told his dad when he returned my card. "You've been here sneering and judging through two whiskeys. You're done. I'll anxiously await your next judgment visit, but for now you need to go."

Dick crossed his arms and lifted his chin. "And if I don't?"

Bode shrugged. "I call the cops and have you removed."

Dick sputtered and muttered, seething with anger and just a bit tipsy. "Just like you to have to rely on cops to do your dirty work. A real man wouldn't need to turn to the law to keep his business running."

Bode leaned on the bar, only inches from his father. "A real man wouldn't criticize and condemn his sons for their sexuality and their job choices. I'm tired of your attitude, your presence in my life, and your constant fault-finding, old man. Leave. Now."

Dick put a nickel on the bar. "'Bout all the whole lot of you are worth," he said with disdain before turning to leave.

"Fuck, I'm sorry," Bode said and blew out a breath. "I knew he was out here—was letting him drink until he got bored. Was he terrible?"

"Nah, just told me I should leave Gabe so he can find someone better than a mechanic."

Bode's eyes went wide for a fraction of a second before

his face contorted with anger. "Don't you listen to him. You and Gabe are amazing people on your own, but together you absolutely shine. Don't you ever take anything my dad says to heart. He's an angry, spiteful, bigot who has nothing better to do than try to make everyone as miserable as him."

Angry and shaken up by the run-in with Dick, I could only nod and pick up my to-go bag. "Thanks man. Appreciate it."

Bode cocked a brow. "I'm serious. Don't take anything he says to heart. He's a douche. I've had my entire life to figure that out—and he still gets to me from time to time —shake it off. What you and my brother have is real. Don't ever think less of yourself or less of your relationship because of what some burned-out asshole bigot says." He slapped a hand on my shoulder. "Plus, I don't want you to make me have to pull out the *you hurt my brother and I'll have to kill you* act."

I smiled slightly. "Gotcha. Thanks. Better get this to Gabe, he'll be hangry soon."

The whole walk back to the shop, my mind was racing a million miles a minute. First Jeanie, then Josh, now Dick. Three instances where I was made to feel what I had with Gabe was wrong—wrong in general, wrong for me, and wrong for him. My heart clenched. If what we had was truly bad for Gabe, I'd let him go in a heartbeat if it meant doing what was best for him. But I couldn't actually wrap my head around anything Gabe and I had together being wrong. Maybe I was blinded by my love for him, maybe I just didn't want to see it. Would we both be better off if I let him go? I rubbed my aching chest. Perhaps Gabe would be better off, but I knew I'd never recover. Was that a selfish dick move on my part to stay with him just so *I* wouldn't hurt?

I climbed the steps to Gabe's place, my heart heavy, my brain scrambled, and wondering what in the world I should do with all the shit in my head right then.

"What's wrong?" Gabe asked the moment I walked in the door.

I hugged him close, kissed him gently, and pressed my forehead against his. "Let's eat. I need to process a couple things, then we'll talk. Okay?" I hadn't been sure I was ready to talk to Gabe about the conversations with Josh and Dick, but the moment I saw him, I knew that talking it out was the best plan. He'd taught me that keeping the feelings bottled up did no one any good.

"Oookaaay," Gabe drawled, "but *we'll talk* seems ominous."

I kissed him again. "We're good. We'll talk. I learned from someone pretty smart that working through feelings is the best thing for a person."

We ate our food while Gabe shared stories of his three days at work. Jeanie had continued with the drama until Dr. Renner had threatened to call the police to have her removed. She'd left ranting and raving about depravity and law suits. Eden had started treatments and so far, hadn't been hit with very many side effects. The day before had been a pitch-in at the office so Gabe spoke of the delicious and not so delicious offerings he'd had to choose from.

He asked me about the bikes I'd worked on. I knew he didn't know half of what I was talking about, but it made me happy that he wanted to hear about my work. He was anxious to ride on my bike, and I promised we'd take a ride once it wasn't so cold. Riding a motorcycle in the cold was doable, but it wasn't always a lot of fun, especially if a person didn't have the right equipment. I wanted his first time on a motorcycle to be enjoyable so he'd want to go again and again. I had these crazy dreams of Gabe and me just loading up and driving off with no particular destination in mind, spending the day soaking up the sun and enjoying the scenery, discovering little towns, and eventually returning to Indy exhausted but happy and content.

"Okay, I can't chit-chat any longer. You're killing me with the *we'll talk* shit. Let's go, spit it out, let's talk," Gabe rambled, his anxiety evident.

I pulled him to the couch and took his hands in mine. "A couple things have happened and they've got my head and heart pulled in about a thousand directions. I'm going to tell you about some run-ins I had with Josh and your dad."

Gabe's eyes went wide before they flashed with anger.

I held up a hand. "I need you to know that I've thought over what they said. On one hand, I had convinced myself they were right and decided I was being unfair to you— decided I should let you go—but on the other hand…"

"Unless your other damn hand says you realized you're being a complete fool listening to any fucking thing those two douchebag dicks have to say, I swear to God I will find them and bitch slap them both until you agree that *nothing* they say has *anything* to do with us." Gabe launched himself from the couch. "I can't believe you'd let anything they'd say sway you. Holy shit, Danny! I thought we had something but you're letting some bullshit my cheating asshole ex and my absent asshole father spew make you question us? You're going to leave me because Josh tells you I'm too gay? Because he tells you I'll get clingy? Break up with me because my dad tells you I'm a disappointment? Well, fuck that shit, Danny. Fuck that! And I'll tell you something else…"

I stood, wrapped an arm around his waist, and yanked him close, capturing his lips with mine, kissing him hard and deep until he whimpered against my mouth. "You done?" I asked.

"Maybe," Gabe quipped, still fiery. "It depends on what you have to say. If you're going to say *anything* about us breaking up because of something those two fuckheads said, I've got more to say."

"As I was saying," I began, "before *someone* interrupted, I was torn. Part of me let them get to me, get in my head, make me question myself and wonder if maybe I was being unfair to you. Do you deserve to be strapped to nothing more than a mechanic? Someone who will maybe, deep down, always be *Murder*?"

Gabe started to protest, but I kissed him quiet again.

"But then I realized, I can't let you go. *Won't* let you go. I won't give up on us. I'll prove I'm not Murder. I'll prove Josh, Dick, Jeanie, and *all* the fuckers out there that they're wrong. Prove that what you and I have—individually *and* together—is real and right."

Gabe's face softened and he smiled. "Go on, I have no rebuttal at this time."

I kissed him, cupping his face in my hands, and pressed my forehead against his. In a gruff whisper, I continued, "I didn't know I needed you. Convinced myself I was fine; alone was better—pushing aside feelings and longings was for the best. Then you came along with those damn blue eyes and beautiful smile. You didn't try to change me, didn't say I was wrong or worthless. You met me where I was, and day-by-day—maybe without even knowing, just by being you—you drew me from my murky darkness into the light." Closing my eyes and breathing Gabe in deeply, I just held him for a moment. "I'm sorry I let them get to me. I'm sorry I made you think I would *ever* throw away what we have. If you ever need better, you let me know…"

Gabe squawked, but I kept on.

"But until—and *if* that ever happens—I will continue to love you, support you, fight for us, and keep working to make myself better."

Gabe blinked watery eyes. "*You* make *me* better. We make each other better. I love you—both Danny and Murder, the good, the painful, the present, the past—and we don't have room in our lives for people like Jeanie or Josh or even my dad. If he ever gets his head out of his ass and becomes a better person maybe—but let's face it, I don't see that ever happening—until then he has no place in my life. Josh was barely a blip on the map of my life and he gave up *any* chance of being part of my present or future. People like Jeanie are out there. They suck, but we'll have to deal with it." He kissed me, his arms snaked around my neck. "We do what's best for us. We surround ourselves with our chosen circle, our found family, we love each other, we grow together, we accept our faults and push each other to reach for our best, always. But we never let the negativity drive a wedge between us."

I nodded and we stood in the living room holding each other for several moments. A weight had been lifted from me the moment my head and heart stopped fighting it and realized letting Gabe go was the most ridiculous idea I'd *ever* let people push on me. The old Danny—*Murder* —would have simmered and stewed, broken things off, pushed aside the heartache and hurt. I was glad to tell the old me goodbye.

"You in the mood for something sexy?" Gabe whispered.

"As long as you're involved, yes. Always yes." I ran my hands down his back and cupped his ass.

"Well, I *may* have ordered a sexy pair of lace panties that are too big for me but would fit you just perfectly." He swayed his hips and ran his hands lightly over my chest, his thumbs teasing my nipples. "I have this image of you in black lace and your black work boots, nothing else."

I was rock-hard already, my cock totally on board with the idea. "I guess it depends on whether or not you'd be joining me in this little impromptu fashion show."

Gabe bit his lip and batted his lashes. "I may have bought a new pair of red lace. *And*," he drawled, "I have a pair of red heels in the back of my closet that would look amazing with the lace, if you're okay with that?"

"My hot-as-fuck boyfriend in red lace panties and heels while I'm in black lace and boots? It's like my own little kinky porn scene come true," I teased. "I'm in, *so* in."

"Go to the bathroom. The panties are in a bag on the sink. Come to the bedroom in just the lace and boots." Gabe kissed me and swatted my ass as I walked away.

A few minutes later, feeling a strange mixture of desire and confidence mixed with anxiety and unsureness, I walked into Gabe's bedroom and nearly swallowed my tongue. He stood facing the bed, a sultry look thrown over his shoulder, his ass cupped perfectly in red lace, and the red heels accentuating the muscles in his long, slender legs.

"Holy fuck," I growled and started toward him.

But Gabe turned to face me and I stopped. The front was just as gorgeous. The red lace bulging, his V on display as if pointing to the promised land. He licked his lips and trailed his eyes from my unlaced black boots to the skimpy black lace underwear. I knew my cock was on complete display—I'd had issues getting myself stuffed into the material even though it was made for a dick and balls. Gabe made a motion telling me to turn around.

I obeyed. I'd checked my ass in the bathroom mirror, I knew it looked *good*.

"Come here," Gabe ordered.

I walked to him and he positioned us in front of his full-length mirror. My legs spread, him standing slightly to my right so the black lace could be seen. The image staring back at us was pure fantasy overload. My wide stance, black lace, black boots, and tattoos contrasted perfectly with the red lace, Gabe's thin waist, and his shiny red heels.

"We're perfect. I'd give anything for a picture of this," Gabe whispered.

"So, take one," I suggested.

Gabe turned to me. "Really?"

"Sure, we're adults. We're not going to put it on social media or use it to blackmail each other. I'd love to have this in the hidden pics on my phone—for my eyes only when I jack off on nights you're not in my bed."

Gabe groaned but grabbed his phone.

And that's how we ended up taking multiple sexy

shots of the two of us clad only in lace, boots, and heels. The pose in front of the mirror was amazing, but we got really creative after a while. Thank goodness for the timer feature on the phone camera. The sexiest part of the pics —aside from just seeing me and Gabe together—was the way we made sure the black and red lace, boots, and heels were always in the shot. Gabe on his knees in front of me. Gabe straddling my hips. Me straddling Gabe's chest. Both of us standing, wrapped in an embrace, my hands splayed across his back and ass. Gabe's back to my front, arms stretched up to wrap around my neck, my hands spread across his chest and abdomen. Me stretched out on the couch, Gabe crawling up my body, his hand brushing the waist of my underwear. Gabe on all fours, looking at the camera while I held his hips from behind. Gabe's legs spread wide, me nestled between his thighs. Both of us stretched out on our sides, my arms around him, kissing his cheek, his eyes closed and a smile on his beautiful face.

We weren't professionals, but the pics turned out great. They may have been for our eyes only, but I absolutely loved them. If ever I had doubts that what had grown between Gabe and me was perfect, a glance at the pics would prove me wrong. The love and connection between us screamed from the screen. The sexual attraction was also clear.

When we finally lost our shoes, I dropped to my knees to slide the lace from Gabe's body, placing kisses on his abs, his hip bones, and teasing his cock with a light swipe of my tongue. Then I stood, shimmied out of the black lace, and pushed him onto the bed.

A very eager Gabe scrambled to the middle of the bed

and shoved a pillow under his ass. "Need you in me," he whispered.

I fumbled in the drawer until I had the lube, slicked myself, and lifted Gabe's legs so he could grab behind his knees. Pressing against his hole, I went slowly knowing we hadn't prepped his muscles at all. Gabe's body opened as he whimpered and panted under me. When I was finally fully inside, Gabe wrapped his legs around my waist and his arms around my neck, and I dropped to my elbows. I began a hard but slow rhythm, thrusting into him hard and deep, pulling out ever-so-slowly, and pumping my hips forcefully again as he made little moaning noises with each thrust.

Pushing up onto my hands, I lifted to separate our chests. Gabe's long, hard cock leaked onto his belly, begging to be touched. "You want to jack yourself or let me come and then you can fuck me?"

"Wanna come in your ass after you fill me," Gabe whined as he writhed under me.

I increased my thrusts, loving every little noise Gabe made each time I reached that spot deep inside. When he scraped his nails down my back and grabbed my ass, my release roared through me and hot cum pulsed into him over and over.

"My turn," Gabe demanded.

I pulled my still throbbing dick from his tight hole and rolled over. Gabe knelt between my knees, reached behind to gather cum and lube from his ass, and coated his dick. He groaned as he slicked the mixture on his cock. "This won't last long at all," he warned as he smeared my hole with the extra. Pressing his head against my entrance, Gabe breached me slowly, feeding his length into me inch by glorious inch. The stretch and sting were almost too much, but when Gabe began to slide in and out, I relaxed and watched his beautiful face.

"Come in me," I whispered, holding my legs open as he thrust over and over. "Fill me."

Gabe tensed and cried out, his final thrust burying him deep inside as his cock pulsed and spilled his release. Despite my earlier orgasm, my ass clenched, milking him for every last drop.

When we'd regained our senses, I grabbed a cloth for clean-up. We fell asleep cuddled together and I'd never been happier that I'd decided not to let the words of people who weren't at all important separate Gabe and me.

9

GABE

THE NEXT MORNING, Danny and I spent a bit of extra time in bed before showering and starting the day. He had three appointments in the shop. I had a volunteer gig at Rose Gardens and had promised Ginny I'd drop in.

Danny was going to meet me at The Salty Lizard later, but I was doing dinner with Bode, Benji, and Kyson first. Significant others were showing up after for drinks.

With a long hug, sweet kiss, and exchange of *I love you*, Danny headed down to the shop and I hopped into my car to head to Rose Gardens.

I adored being a nurse. Most of the time. Loved my patients, loved being able to take care and assist. But the volunteer position was a breath of fresh air. I enjoyed the kids at the practice, but the elderly folks were just as enjoyable in a different way. I liked volunteering because none of the medical stuff was on me. I could just sit and listen, chat, read with them instead of worrying about medicine and stats and diagnosis and prognosis. But the staff loved having a licensed nurse volunteering because I could help watch for issues if someone wasn't doing well. For the most part, I liked pediatrics the best because kids had their whole lives ahead of them—unless I hit painful brick walls when patients like Eden got devastating news —but the older people were nearing the end and that always made me sad. Volunteering made me feel like I could at least bring them some happiness as they enjoyed their twilight years.

I pulled up at Rose Gardens at the exact same time as Chase.

"Hey, man. Good to see you," Chase said as we walked toward the facility. "You volunteering today?"

"Yep, going to make a couple visits and then Ginny made me promise I'd come see her. You going to be here for a while?"

Chase held up a bag and a drink carrier. "She ordered breakfast. I'm off today so I'll likely stay all day. When she naps, I'll nap." He chuckled before sobering. "Love her and love visiting, but I always get anxious walking in here. Never know if it's a good day or bad day. Then I feel guilty because *I'm* not the one with cancer so what type of day she's having isn't really my place to feel anxious over—I just want her comfortable. It's not something I've been tracking, but it's beginning to feel like the bad days have been happening more often—or maybe they are just taking longer for her to bounce back from." He blew a breath out of puffed cheeks. "Seems like I just got her back, my sister needs her mom—don't get me wrong, Bode and Sage are fabulous parents—but I don't want Rosie losing Ginny any time soon. Is there ever a good time for a kid to lose their mother?"

I smiled sadly as we reached the door. "Speaking from

personal experience, no there's definitely never a good time. Rosie is lucky to have Bode and Sage *and* her brother to support her. You and Xan are great with Rosie—with all the kids." We walked into the foyer and signed in. I took the list the receptionist gave me for who may be most in need of visits before walking with Chase toward Ginny's room. "Ginny's cancer has been progressing for a very long time, even longer than she's known about it probably, but it's a slow growing one. I don't know that *lucky* and *cancer* go in the same sentence, but I know she considers herself lucky to have had such a long stretch of time to spend with you and Rosie."

"When she told me she opted out of any kind of treatment, I wanted to argue and tell her no, tell her she had to fight, she couldn't just give up," Chase said quietly as we walked down the hall. "But I realize now she gave herself and the rest of us a gift with that choice. Treatment *maybe* would have given her some more time, but she very likely would have been so sick during that time that we wouldn't have been able to be around her because of germs and whatnot. I'm so grateful for the time with her—just wish we weren't on a limited plan."

"I get that. But really, we're *all* on a limited time plan. There are no guarantees. You're making the most of the time she has and that's what's important." We reached Ginny's door and Chase knocked.

"Special delivery," he called.

"Come in, come in," Ginny answered as she opened the door. "Coffee!"

Chase laughed as he handed over the drink carrier. "Yes, coffee. The good kind, just like you ordered. Good to see you, too," he teased.

"Oh, yes, yes," Ginny tsked. "Always great to see my favorite nephew-turned-son. But the coffee in this place is *not* up to par. I'm sure my payments go for *a lot* of great things here, but they definitely aren't spending it on good coffee."

"I brought you a bag so you can make your own," Chase said as he pulled the vacuum-sealed pack of coffee from the bag of goodies. "Plus, a breakfast sandwich and pastry."

I accepted the donut Chase offered, visited for a moment, and then said goodbye with the promise of coming back later.

"Don't let any of those old people convince you to stay longer. I *need* my Gabe time," Ginny scolded.

Three hours later, I texted Chase to be sure he and Ginny were awake, and headed toward her room where I'd end my volunteer shift.

"It's about time you got back," Ginny chided with a grin. "Chase and I are so bored we had to resort to naps."

We settled in Ginny's tiny living area with hot tea for all.

"How's little Eden doing?" Ginny asked.

"She's still got a long road, but her aunt told one of our nurses that Eden's doctor said her first round of treatment went very well, her numbers look amazing, and he's expecting remission to happen fairly quickly."

"That's just wonderful," Ginny exclaimed. "I hate that she and her family have to go through this, but I love hearing the great outlook."

We chatted about random things for a while, laughing about this and that, and just enjoying our time together.

Chase showed Ginny several pictures and videos of Rosie and Oliver.

When the chatter paused for a moment, Ginny took a sip of her tea. "Boys, I need you to know that I have a feeling deep in my heart that my time is near." She held up a hand when Chase and I startled. "I don't mean a day or two, nothing like that. But I have this feeling I'll be gone within a year," Ginny stated very matter-of-factly.

Chase took her hand. I saw that he wanted to argue, tell her she was wrong, but he kept quiet and just listened.

"I'm not telling you all of this to be dramatic or bring you down," Ginny said with a wave of her hand. "My point is just to let you know that I plan to live every day to the fullest—I feel like I've been doing a great job of that so far. I want to build memories with Chase and Rosie. Dance, laugh, enjoy delicious food, love on my friends and family, I want to do it all." She took another sip. "My bad days are getting a bit worse here and there, there's no denying that. But I'll keep fighting until I don't have one more breath. I've never regretted my decision to forgo treatment and I'm blessed by every single moment I've been given. I want you boys to be part of carrying on my memory."

My eyes stung with tears and I couldn't hide my sniffle.

Chase put an arm around his aunt.

"Make sure you tell Rosie all about me, how much I loved her, share stories about me, laugh about my crazy past and the ridiculousness Millie and I have gotten up to." She patted Chase's leg. "The way I want to be honored is for you to love in my name. Love your friends, love yourselves, love your partners. Do it for you first, but remember me in all of your love. There's no guarantee, I get that, but I have high hopes for happily ever after for all of you. Chase and Xan, Ty and Vic, Gabe and Danny, all the Silvers—my heart is fully invested in your love and futures. There's nothing I enjoy more than a good love story—whether it's friendship or family or romantic love. Keep my memory alive through your love. That's what I ask."

Tears spilled from my eyes and I knew Chase was wiping away his own.

"Now, there's no reason for tears. I plan to be here as long as possible and make the most of every day. I just needed my two best boys to hear my wishes. Millie knows as well. I'll write letters for Rosie—Bode and Sage will keep me alive in her heart, I know that—and you, too, Chase. But until then, I want love and happiness and joy and fun to fill our lives."

Chase and I dried our eyes and listened to Ginny spin a tale of how she and Millie flirted with two residents down the hall but got busted and sent back to her room before anything *sexy* could happen.

By the time Chase and I gave Ginny big hugs and headed out, I was emotionally zapped.

"That was rough," Chase said raggedly.

"Yeah, it was. You good?"

He nodded. "Yeah, gonna get home and share with Xan. Maybe go to The Lizard later for drinks to chill out."

"Sounds good. I'm meeting my brothers and cousin for dinner. We'll all be there drinking later. Come on by and join us."

I slapped Chase on the back and headed home to change for dinner.

* * *

I walked into The Salty Lizard later feeling excited about dinner, but also off-kilter. It was so surreal to have been an *only* child my whole life and then find two brothers and a cousin. I knew stories like mine didn't always work out in a positive way and I was lucky that mine seemed headed toward a happy ending, at least with my siblings. My father was a different beast all together. I frowned at the thought of Dick Silver—and Rod Silver, an uncle I hadn't even met—as I approached the back table where Bode, Benji, and Kyson were already seated.

"I swear to God, if Danny broke up with you because of what Dad said, I'm going to kick both of their asses," Bode growled.

My eyes went wide. "What? No, he didn't." I pulled out a chair and sat down.

Bode softened. "Sorry, you had a look on your face and I was worried Danny let Dick get to him. I tried to talk to him when I saw Dad was at the bar talking to him, but I wasn't sure if I got through to him. Dad can be an absolute shit when he wants to weasel his way into someone's mind and Danny looked as if he'd been ambushed something fierce."

"Oh, no. I *was* thinking about Daddy Dearest so that's probably the look you saw, but Danny didn't break up with me." I said hello to Sage when he brought waters and took our drink orders. He was joining us later, after our *bro time* as Bode called it. "Although, Danny's head took quite a beating between Dick and my ex."

"Your ex?" Bode asked.

"Yeah, we went to Ash & Elm the other day and my ex, Josh, was there. I guess he confronted Danny when I went to the restroom. Told him about how I'm *too gay*, too clingy and needy, how I've got unacceptable kinks, how I'm embarrassing in front of friends. That type of shit." I sipped my water before taking a deep breath. I was still so pissed at Josh and had half a mind to call him—or at least confront him if I ever saw him again—but on the other hand, I didn't want to waste any more time on him—he was a regrettable past, I wanted to enjoy now and look toward the future. "Danny was pissed. Then Dick was in the bar. Between the two of them, Danny got an earful. Honestly, he was waffling for a bit—they got in his mind pretty good—thinking he wasn't good enough for me, that he needed to let me go so I had a fair shot at something better, that kind of shit."

"But he changed his mind?" Benji asked.

I mulled over the question for a moment. "Not so much *changed* his mind because he hadn't decided to break it off, just realized that the thoughts Josh and Dick had put in his head were ridiculous."

"That's good. You guys talked it all out?" Kyson asked.

"Yeah, it's amazing how a guy I could barely pull two words from when we first met can now have entire *long* conversations—involving feelings even—these days. He's opened up so much—a far cry from the man I met as *Murder* such a short time ago." I smiled softly as I thought of Danny and how much he meant to me.

"Probably has you to thank for that. You've changed him," Kyson said.

"I don't think I *changed* him so much—and honestly, I didn't meet him and set a goal to change him. I liked him just fine the way he was. I think the words and feelings have always been there, he just never thought anyone would care to hear them, never wanted to deal with all that could result from the feelings—when you let feelings loose with no one there to help you cope it can get nasty. Growing up with indifferent parents, losing them to a violent crime, being rumored to be involved in their deaths, thrown to the wolves with a mean-ass uncle—well, it's no surprise he thought no one wanted to hear what he had to say, no one cared about what he was feeling." My chest hurt every time I thought of what Danny had been through. "He just needed someone to let him know it was okay to share." I shrugged, but my heart warmed thinking of how Danny had grown to trust me with his words and feelings.

"Well, I'm not sure just anyone could have done that for him. He's been around Bay for a long time and never said a lot. He's known some of us for a while and he's just never been a talker. I liked the guy from the beginning— just a gut feeling—but he was always quiet, angry, and brooding. You brought him out of that whether it was your plan or not." Bode slapped the back of his hand against my shoulder.

"I think the best thing you ever did for him was refuse to call him Murder," Kyson chimed in. "I hate that none of us ever thought to wonder about the nickname and consider that it may have had negativity attached to it."

"Yeah, we're all a bunch of dumbasses for not thinking

the name *Murder* was maybe from a negative past," Benji grumbled while rolling his eyes. "That was a total fail on our part. I honestly had never seen the guy smile until he met you and now he's nearly beaming every damned time I see him. You're definitely his person, not sure two people more different have ever clicked so quickly and perfectly, but you two made it look easy."

"Just because the three of us fought our relationships tooth and nail," Bode gestured around the table, "doesn't mean things can't click easily."

Kyson held up a hand. "Whoa, don't include me in that. *I* didn't fight things with Bay. That was all his doing."

Benji crossed his arms over his chest. "To be fair, Rhys and I didn't have the most traditional of beginnings. We had a lot to work through. We fought it for a reason—a stupid reason in hindsight, but we thought we were doing the right thing at the time."

Bode narrowed his eyes. "Fine, maybe *I* was the one who fought my relationship tooth and nail," he grumbled just as Sage walked up.

"Oh, did you ever," Sage drawled. "This man," he squeezed Bode's shoulder, "bitched and moaned, thought up every damn excuse imaginable, and pushed, pushed, pushed trying to fight against the spark between us." He cocked his head with a smile and put his hand on his hip. "But I eventually wore him down. Once he got a taste— okay, even with a taste he was still fighting it—but after a while he finally gave in."

"Those two," Kyson tipped his glass toward Bode and Sage, "were something to watch for sure. Sage, innocent, inexperienced, smart as hell *kid* walks in and Bode's life was turned upside down. It got frustrating watching him trying to protest and reason his way out of liking Sage, but it was entertaining. I think we all breathed a little easier when Bode finally pulled his head from his ass."

"Yeah, yeah, I took a bit of time to come around," Bode grumbled. "But it's all good now. Relationships start in all kinds of ways. I'm not saying one is better than the other, I was just saying that Gabe and Danny made it look easy."

"All right, boys, what do you want to eat? I need to get your orders in before we get slammed." Sage tapped his pen on a tiny notebook. "After the first wave of dinner rush, I've got two coming in to take my place so I can join you. Don't use up all the stories and laughs before I get here."

We ordered our food. I was crazy excited about my burger and fries—with fry sauce of course—but I was mostly looking forward to the Brussels sprouts. Absolute best dish they served at The Lizard—and that was saying a lot because all of their food was delicious. The foodie in me was in hog heaven every time I got to eat truly great food.

"So, we want to plan a trip down to the farm," Bode began after wrapping an arm around Sage's waist and pulling him close. Sage kissed the top of his head and went off to put in our orders. "I was able to find times when neither of the Porn Brothers would be there, thanks to Mom and Aunt Janet. They said Dick and Rod are traveling a lot lately and we're welcome to visit the farm at any time."

"But we can narrow down a time when Mom and Aunt Debbie won't be there if you'd rather not be around Dick's wife," Kyson added.

Bode and Benji nodded.

"Honestly, if she's okay with me being there, I have no ill-will toward her. She probably has more reason to hate me than me her. I'm the result of her husband's infidelity; I can't imagine that's an easy pill to swallow." It would have been different if Debbie or my brothers had known about me so long ago—if they'd mistreated me or my mom, maybe I'd have bad feelings toward Debbie, but that wasn't the case.

"Then let's get a trip set up. We'll all go." Benji gestured around the table. "Partners too, of course. Kids and dogs as well. I know Mom and Aunt Janet will be thrilled to have the kids for the weekend, and the dogs love to run. And our mom isn't the type to blame you—or even Violet—for my dad's infidelity. From some of what she's said over the years, I'm pretty sure both Dick and Rod have trouble keeping it in their pants when they're on business trips." Benji wrinkled his nose. "She has no bad feelings toward you. Any bad feelings she has definitely are directed at Dad—rightfully so."

"We could invite Chase, Xan, Ty, and Vic to come down on either Friday or Saturday night for a big bonfire. If we wait a few weeks, we can maybe pick a weekend that's not *terribly* cold. Plus, a big fire will keep us warm," Kyson suggested.

It was decided that we'd pick a weekend based on weather and schedules and get the whole trip planned. Spring Break was an option since the kids would be out of school and none of our crew was heading on vacation at that point.

"I'm really sorry Dick cornered Danny at the bar," Bode grumbled. "I know you have to get to know him and decide for yourself what type of person he is, but I want to protect you from his venomous bite, and the way he went after your boyfriend was shit."

"I had high hopes the first time I met him. The fact that he came to my graduation when I invited him made me think he was ready to know me. Within five minutes of talking to him, all of those dreams were dashed for sure. In hindsight, I was deluding myself to think that a man who had never once been in contact with me would suddenly show up and shower me with all the years of fatherly love and support I'd been missing." I rolled my eyes at past Gabe's stupidity. "I think I always hoped there was a chance he didn't know about me. He sent Mom away with money for an abortion so there was always that chance. Knowing what I know about Dick now, I'm sure he kept tabs on Mom and me. I bet it pissed him off that she didn't get rid of me, but as long as she wasn't asking for anything from him, he just went on with his life pretending I didn't exist."

Bode clenched his fist. "The part that pisses me off the most is that he kept you from us all that time. We would have adored having a baby brother, even if you could only visit from time to time. Seriously, all three of us have issues with our fathers, but Dad and I have always gone at it the most. This is just one more reason for me to keep him out of my life."

"I mean, if Dad would have introduced us to you, it would have caused some drama with Mom and Dad," Benji stated, "but they've never had the best marriage. The older I get, the more I wonder what in the world keeps Mom and Aunt Janet with Dick and Rod. I know they use the money that comes with their marriages for lots of charities and community work—and I know our moms have allocated *a lot* of the money our dads make to the horses and property because those things also mean a lot to them—but I hate they've stayed with assholes for so long. I think at first it was likely a 'for the kids' type thing. Dick and Rod always had Mom and Aunt Janet home doing their *wifely* duties and only really *allowed* them to do charities if it brought good publicity—not that we realized these things until we were much older. I think our moms probably got to a point where they realized they didn't really have the skills needed to move into the job world, so they used a hefty portion of our dads' money to fund charities and keep themselves busy. I'm not sure how Mom would have taken to finding out about Dad's affair and child back then. But I know she's completely open to it now—well, to the point where she's not angry with you. With Dad? Yeah, I think it's just one more item on the list of his grievances. And I doubt she blames Violet—I'm sure Dad didn't say, 'Hey, I'm married, want to have an affair?'"

"I would have hated to hurt your mom with my presence all those years ago. And I would have hated leaving *my* mom alone to go off to hang with my *other* family. I don't know that a younger me would have been able to brush off Dick's words and attitude." I put ketchup on the burger Sage had placed in front of me and then popped a fry in my mouth. "I would have loved to know you all back then—all I ever wanted was siblings to play with—but I think it all kinda worked out for the best." I groaned as I chewed a savory Brussels sprout. "Seriously, these damn things are so good. I wish I could fix them this perfectly."

Bode winked and smiled. "Secret recipe. You'll just have to keep coming here to get your fix."

"That's how he keeps Xan and Chase coming in with the fry sauce." Benji chuckled. "Well, that and Chase wants his paycheck."

"Honestly, I sometimes think Chase would work just for the chance at tips and talking to customers. The kid is totally in his element here." Bode popped a cheese-covered tater tot in his mouth. "I don't *expect* him to work here his whole life, but he's damn good at what he does and I'd be happy to have him here for as long as he wants to be."

When dinner finished, we pulled two more small tables to the corner and set up for the rest of the crew to join us.

As we settled back into our seats, the back of my neck tingled. I turned toward the door just in time to see Danny walk in, tight black t-shirt under a black leather jacket, worn jeans, black boots loosely laced, and a smile meant all for me. He sat down, put an arm around me, and pulled me close. "Is it crazy that I missed you today?"

I turned and kissed his cheek, smelling his soap and shampoo from a recent shower. "Not at all. I missed you, too. You smell good and you look fantastic. Good enough to eat," I whispered.

Danny put his mouth to my ear. "I may or may not have slipped on a certain pair of black lace underwear," he teased. "You'll have to find out later."

"Not fair," I whined.

As more people began to fill the table, Danny grabbed drinks for us and we settled in for small talk with friends. I sat leaning into Danny as his arm rested across my shoulders and watched our crew while making several observations.

First, I now had a *crew*. A group of true friends. Not people I was *trying* to fit in with—I didn't have to change myself to fit with this bunch, they accepted me with no question. Back in college, hell, even just a year ago, I never would have thought I'd get a chance for this type of love and friendship.

Second, there was a lot of bad in the world, but sitting in The Lizard with friends showed me there was also a shit ton of good going on. Every single man at the table was a generous, caring, productive member of society and I was truly blessed to know them, to learn from them, to look up to them. Specifically blessed to be loved by and in love with the man who was protectively wrapping his arm around me while we drank and spent time with friends.

Third, as much as I missed my mom and would have loved to have her healthy and back with me, I was proud of and grateful for my chosen family—I knew Violet would have loved all of them. I'd heard people talk about their *found family* and never really got it—until I met this group. I had my core of Danny, Bode, Benji, and Kyson—yes, my brothers and cousin were blood-relations, but we'd all *chosen* to be in each other's lives. Then I had Sage, Rhys, and Bay—they were natural choices as the partners of the other three. I appreciated having established couples to turn to as Danny and I forged into our new relationship— we were building our own unique situation and I wasn't trying to copy off anyone, but having good, loving relationship role models to look to was a huge help. Having more chosen family in Ty and Vic, Chase and Xan just made my life even fuller and better. When I added in Millie, Ginny, and the kids, plus a couple people I was close to at work, I saw that I was truly blessed with my chosen family. Meeting them and being welcomed with open arms made me realize how much I'd been missing with the superficial, generic friendships I had in high school and college.

We spent the rest of the evening drinking, laughing, and enjoying our time together. Talk of the trip down to the Silver farm sparked plans for a future group trip to Disney and I made a note to start saving for that absolute *must-have* trip. I'd never been to Disney and it was definitely something I wanted to experience with Danny and my family.

"*Sixteen* people traveling to Disney? On a plane? In a hotel?" Danny's panicked whisper tickled my ear. "That sounds like an absolute nightmare. I'm going to need therapy and Xanax. Before *and* after."

I chuckled. "We won't have to have *all* sixteen seats together or six adjoining rooms. But it would be so much fun to watch the kids meet the characters and ride the rides. We could go off on our own, but the option of character dinners and parades and shows with the whole group sounds kinda fun to me."

Danny narrowed his eyes at me. "*The kids* meeting the characters, riding the rides, watching the parade, and seeing shows? The kids are the ones you're mostly thinking of, right?" He smirked and raised a brow to wait for my answer.

I bit my lip to hold back a smile. "Fine, I'd be lying if I said I wasn't super excited about all of that for me, too. Mom and I never got to do big vacations like that. I have the means now, I have family to enjoy it with, I definitely want to experience it."

"Fine," Danny relented. "I'm in—not kidding about the need for Xanax though—but at some point during the vacation, I want to see you dressed in nothing but Mickey ears."

My hand brushed over his crotch as I leaned closer to whisper, "Maybe I'll find a mouse tail butt plug to complete the look, that could be all kinds of fun."

"Jesus," Danny growled.

We kept up the teasing throughout the rest of the evening as we enjoyed our time with friends and family.

"We're going to call it a night," Bay said. "We've got Mom with the kids so we should get home. Let's make plans to have dinner with Millie and Ginny within the next week. Love these guys' nights, but those two ladies add a special touch to our get-togethers."

"If by special touch you mean inappropriate hilarity, you're very right," Vic commented.

"Millie told us Kyson had to explain what Netflix and chill was so she'd stop asking if you guys wanted to Netflix and chill with her." Danny snorted at the look of horror on Bay's face.

"She was so cute," Kyson said. "*I was just wondering if you boys wanted to do some Netflix and chill next time I come over.* After she said it three or four times, I had to explain it. I couldn't let her keep going that way."

"Well, she gets it now. Told us the other day that if she ever found a man to keep up with her, he better be ready for Netflix and chill—not the movie and napping kind— because *good dick is hard to find*," I said, barely able to tell the story without laughing.

Chase nearly choked.

"Don't worry, Ginny chimed in at that point to quip *and hard dick is good to find*," Danny added.

"Well, boys, she's not wrong," Bode teased and everyone groaned.

"And with that, we're out," Chase said as he took a final drink.

We all laughed and began the process of saying goodbye, leaving money on the table amidst Bode's protests, pushing tables back where they belonged, and pulling on jackets.

By the time Danny and I reached my place, I was about to jump out of my skin wondering if he'd really put the black lace panties back on. Once upstairs, I kicked off my shoes, threw my jacket somewhere close to the hook, and ran my hands up Danny's torso to his shoulders to push the leather from his body.

"You in a hurry?" Danny teased as he leaned in to kiss me.

"You know I am. I want to see if you've got the panties on," I whispered against his mouth. "Take off your shoes," I demanded as his jacket fell to the floor.

Danny toed off his boots and followed me to my bed. "So, prediction? Am I wearing them or not? Was it all just a tease?"

I pursed my lips and tapped my chin. "At this point, I just wanna swallow your cock so I'm not too concerned. But, I'm going with no on the underwear. I think you were just kidding." I popped open his button, slid the zipper down, and slid my hands around to cup his ass. His very bare ass. "Commando?" I growled.

"The lace had dried cum stains. I really was planning

to wear them, but when I realized they needed to be washed, I decided bare was just as good." Danny leaned down and kissed my neck, biting at the sensitive skin. "Now, I believe you said something about swallowing my cock?"

"Hmmm," my head dropped back, offering Danny more access, "did I? I don't recall."

"Well, one of us needs to be on our knees soon. I don't care who goes first, but I've got my own plans to be face-fucked so someone needs to get busy." Danny rocked his hips into me.

I dropped to my knees, pulling his jeans down as I went. Taking his thick length in my hand, I stroked, licked his head, and teased his balls before taking him deep in my mouth. I loved everything about giving head. The fullness of my mouth, stretch of my lips, taste of his seed, scent of his skin, all of it. When Danny fisted my hair gently and guided my head on his cock, I suddenly wanted everything he could give me as quickly as possible so we could get to the part where I was face-fucking him. I squeezed his balls slightly and worked a wet finger between his cheeks to tease at his hole. Danny groaned and thrust his hips hard, his dick throbbing between my lips as he unloaded on my tongue. With cum dripping from the corner of my mouth, I licked him clean, stood and wiped my mouth with the back of my hand, and pushed my jeans and underwear down.

My long cock sprang up and Danny licked his lips as he climbed onto the bed. With his head against the headboard, he motioned to me to straddle his chest. "Give it to me, fuck my face," he growled.

I fisted my dick and rubbed the wet head along his lips. "Open," I ordered.

Danny obeyed and I fed my entire length between his lips. Lifting up to balance only on my toes and my hands against the headboard, I began to fuck into his mouth. Looking down and watching his nostrils flare as he took every thrust drove me wild and my balls tightened. "Not gonna last," I warned and began to pump my hips harder and faster as Danny's hands gripped my ass and urged me on. My release tore through me and I moaned his name as I erupted deep in his throat.

As I dropped to my knees, my spent cock sliding from his mouth, I chuckled. "Lace or no lace, I love you and I love doing that. Shower?"

Danny gave me a blissed out smile and wiped a drop of cum from the corner of his mouth. "Yeah, then we're going to sleep for a while. Later, we're going to wake and do that again, plus a lot more. Maybe several times before morning."

"Oh yeah?" I teased.

"Yep, definitely." Danny kissed me. "And I've got serious plans to make sure you're in my bed, in my arms, for the rest of our lives."

Tears sprang to my eyes. "For real?" I asked, emotion choking me.

"As long as you'll have me, I want nothing more than to spend the rest of my life loving you—I love everything about you. You will *never* be too much for me. You saved me when I didn't even realize I needed saving, accepted me for who I am, and showed me a love I had never even hoped to have. The rest of our lives should be just about enough time to show you how much I love you."

I swallowed thickly. "I love you," I whispered. "Thank you for loving me with no questions, no complaints, no demands. Coming here, finding my family, finding you, it's been the best thing that's ever happened to me. I'll gladly spend the rest of my life loving you."

Danny hummed sleepily against my neck. "We're going to need several more pairs of panties. Seems my kink is most definitely lace."

"We can order tomorrow." The thought of browsing an online selection of lace panties, modeled by extremely sexy men, with Danny had me anticipating a very hot conclusion as soon as the credit card information was submitted. "But we should shower now before we fall asleep and wake up sticky and gross."

"We're already sticky and gross," Danny joked as he swiped at a bit of cum on my neck.

"Okay, before we wake up stickier and grosser than we already are," I added before slapping his ass. "Come on, let's go. I'm sleepy."

We showered, slow and gentle, and fell into bed. Wrapped in Danny's arms, with the promise of forever and always floating softly between us, we drifted to sleep. I looked forward to waking in Danny's arms—that night, the next morning, and for the rest of our lives.

EPILOGUE

Gabe

THE WEEKEND of our trip to the Silver farm dawned as
perfectly as any spring day ever could. A bite in the
morning air forced all of us into hoodies—Danny and I
layered up even more to ride the bike—and the kids
cuddled with blankets in their car seats. We stopped at
Denny's for breakfast—God bless that waitperson's soul
for taking care of a table of fourteen with smiling grace.
We helped clean the table, left a very large tip, and took
to-go cups of coffee, tea, and chocolate milk with us as we
piled back into our vehicles.

Bode, Sage, Oliver, and Rosie were in Bode's truck.
Bode reported that the kids' constant chatter was possibly
going to lead to his early demise.

Benji, Rhys, Bear, and Brawn were in a truck Rhys
had borrowed from his mom so the dogs could be in

crates in the back while we were in the restaurant. The beasts rode in the extended cab during the drive. The dogs were very happy with the eggs and bacon Benji purchased for them.

"You spoil them," Rhys grumbled.

"You get them each a puppucino every time you go to Starbucks, don't start with me," Benji retorted.

"Touché," Rhys said and they climbed into the truck with two very excited dogs.

I laughed as Cori patted Danny's back while he walked her to the car. The little girl babbled and pointed and laughed, happy to be traveling, thrilled with the pancakes she'd eaten, and content in her buddy Danny's arms. "Okay, in you go," Danny said as he deposited her into her car seat. "I'll see you in a bit." He kissed her nose before Kyson came to strap her in while Bay made sure Arlo was belted properly. Traveling with children was quickly teaching me that nothing was quick or easy and it was *not* for the faint of heart.

My heart melted to see Danny and the little girl together—I wasn't in the *I must have children* boat, but I also wasn't on the *I never want kids* side of the fence. For the time being, I loved my friends' kids—holy hell, I guess they were kinda more like my nieces and nephews—and I adored being around kids all day at the practice, but I wasn't ready to make a decision one way or the other just yet. No need to rush it, I had plenty of children to enjoy and I couldn't help but grin like a fool when I saw my man with a baby.

Danny was Cori's favorite—after her dads, of course— and she was happy in his arms whenever he was around. It was the cutest thing ever, especially since Danny still got that deer-in-the-headlights look anytime Cori made her wishes known that *he* carry her.

Danny tossed me my brand-new helmet. We'd outfitted me with a jacket, boots, and helmet earlier in the week, and Danny had taken me on a few short rides to help me prepare for the two hour drive down to the farm. I *loved* riding on the bike. The speed, the wind in my face, the feeling of Danny's strong thighs between my spread legs, his broad back against my chest, my arms wrapped around him.

I'd teased my hands over him once on a practice ride, but when he nearly ran a stoplight, I'd realized that distracting him when he was trying to drive a very large piece of machinery was probably not the smartest move in the world.

Danny climbed onto the bike and adjusted his helmet and gloves. The engine roared to life and I saw Cori laughing and clapping through the window. She got very excited about motorcycles, probably because she'd been around them in her dad's shop since she was an infant. I waved at her before climbing on behind Danny and tapping his leg to let him know I was good to go. Tap on the right leg, all good. Tap on the left leg, need to stop. Those were our signals.

The drive south was absolutely perfect. I was looking forward to summer rides when the air didn't have the cold bite, but I was warm enough snuggled against Danny. The Indiana spring feel was in the air. Cold mornings, warm sunny days, crisp evenings. But spring in the Midwest was fickle for sure. The weekend before, we'd had temps hovering around freezing. The forecast for the upcoming week was calling for some snow flurries. So, we gratefully grabbed onto the sixty-five-degree temps and sunshine forecast for the weekend and planned to enjoy every moment of our time together.

About two and a half hours later—it was a two-hour drive if you could drive straight through, but coffees, teas, and chocolate milks to-go meant that a potty break was needed for everyone—we pulled onto the Silver property and I was seriously speechless. A long tree-lined lane went down a hill and then forked at the top. Bode had explained he and Benji grew up in the house to the right and Kyson to the left, but they'd spent as much time at each other's houses that it didn't really seem to matter who lived at which house. The fact that the guys had grown up with obvious money—and so very different from me—yet were still some of the most welcoming, generous, kind-hearted, and *good* people I'd ever met, proved to me that their moms were amazing people and having your father's genes didn't automatically mean you had to be the same type of horrible asshole.

Bode had told us to just park in front of the house at first and we'd move vehicles later. I was grateful Bay and Kyson had thrown our bags in their trunk. The saddle bags on Danny's bike held quite a bit more than one would assume at first glance, but they didn't have exactly enough space for both of our clothes. And I was glad to not have the bags strapped on behind me.

Two women came out on the front porch and I was suddenly nervous.

"You okay?" Danny asked.

"Yeah, I'm good. Just worried she's going to hate me. This can't be easy." I took off my gloves and wiped my hands on my jeans.

"Bode and Benji wouldn't have brought you here if she was going to hate you or be rude. They love you," Danny whispered against my ear and wrapped an arm around my shoulders. "You've got this. She's going to love you because they do. She doesn't blame you for Dick's infidelity."

The kids and dogs ran ahead and both women fell right into Grandma mode with hugs and kisses and head pats and ear scratches.

Cori lunged from Kyson's arms toward Danny. His eyes went wide as if he was petrified, but he caught her like a seasoned pro and settled her on his hip with a kiss to her cheek. She pointed toward the house.

"You wanna see your grandma, huh?" Danny asked.

Cori patted the back of his head and laughed.

Once kids, dogs, and baby were properly greeted, Debbie and Janet turned to their sons and sons-in-law for hugs and hellos.

Bode cleared his throat. "We have two more couples coming tonight, but this is Gabe and Danny. Guys, this is my mom, Debbie and my aunt, Janet."

Debbie stepped forward and took my hands in hers. "I'm so very glad to meet you. I'm a firm believer in things working out the way they should—and boy, do we have *a lot* to tell you," she glanced toward her sons, "but I'm so very sorry that Dick's decisions left you without a father when you were younger." She hugged me. "Although, from what my boys have told me, Violet did a kick-ass job raising you. I doubt very much that Dick would have been a good influence." She squeezed my hands. "I would never try to, nor could I ever take the place of your mother. But I want you to know, as my sons' brother, you will always have a place here, a family, and I will love you as my own."

My eyes filled with tears as I choked out a thank you. I hadn't realized how concerned I was about Debbie not accepting me. I'd also not realized how much I'd missed having that motherly love and support in my life. Debbie would never take Mom's place, but knowing she loved and accepted me simply because I was Bode's and Benji's brother meant the world to me.

Janet stepped forward and hugged me. "Same for me. I hate the time we've all missed together, but we're here now and we can move on from here."

"What do you have to tell us?" Benji asked.

Debbie glanced around the porch. "It's already so nice out here. Let's let the kids and dogs play, we'll go to the back deck and we can share. Janet and I will take the kids to the other house after lunch so you boys have this one all to yourselves. We're the babysitters this weekend so Daddy Duty is canceled. We've got it all taken care of."

The look of sheer relief that filled Bode, Sage, Kyson, and Bay's faces would have been comical if it wasn't so serious. They were due for some time off. Being fabulous parents was hard work and they deserved a break.

"We've got Chinese, pizza, and bar-b-que being delivered for lunch if that's all okay," Debbie stated. "We'll split the leftovers between houses."

"Sounds perfect," Kyson said.

We rounded the kids up for bathroom breaks and donning old shoes for playtime, made sure the dogs had food and water—if they ever stopped running around and sniffing everything—and herded everyone to the back of the house. The kids launched themselves at the swing set, the dogs took off to the pond, and Cori squealed with glee when she saw the sand table.

"What's up?" Bode asked, his eyes narrowed.

"Well, Janet and I have spent the better part of the last decade planning to leave your fathers," Debbie cut to the chase. "I'm sorry if you boys grew up thinking your fathers were *good* or *right*. And I'm sorry it took us so long to figure out what to do. I hate that we've had to keep this from your for so long."

Bode, Benji, and Kyson stared at their mothers with wide eyes and slack jaws.

"Go on," Bode said.

"Your fathers were too full of themselves to ever think we'd go against them, so they never checked up on the money we used for keeping the horses and property taken care of, never checked on the charities. Now, don't get me wrong, we poured money—and will continue to—into those things, but we also had a secret account we were slipping money into year after year." Debbie took Janet's hand.

"We've been working with a lawyer for ten years—when we finally came to the conclusion that our marriages were each a farce and the only good thing that came from them were you boys and our abilities to support charities —and earlier this month, we asked Dick and Rod to leave."

I could tell from their expressions that the three boys were shocked.

"Wow, good for you. How did you get the upper hand to keep the houses and property?" Bode asked.

"Well, your fathers were good in their career fields because they were smarmy and the only option around for most people," Debbie said. "*We* found a lawyer who is not only cutthroat and ruthless, he's the best in the state, maybe even the region. We've done everything by the book. There are *a lot* of particulars, but suffice it to say we are well within the law and the houses and property are ours free and clear. Your fathers have a lawyer and he's been in touch, but our guy says there's nothing they can do. A lot of the dumb, conceited decisions your fathers made way back before you boys were born are the ones that worked out best for us and came back to bite them in the ass."

"I'm really glad you guys can finally be rid of them. I'm sorry you had to put up with their shit for so long," Kyson said.

"It's all good. We have our boys," Debbie looked my way, "all *four* of our boys, and we're set. We've got our horses—which we're expanding into a business—and the land, along with our charities. We'll be fine. We had each other the whole time—not sure I could have survived without my best friend by my side, but now we're just looking forward to being grandmas and enjoying the rest of our lives."

"That's an amazing story, I'm happy for you both," I added. "I love when things work out like that. Karma is a real bitch." I barely knew Debbie and Janet, but I already knew I liked them a lot more than Dick and Rod. Maybe I wasn't being fair to Rod. I'd never met the man and I'd heard that he maybe wasn't *as* bad as his brother, but I still liked the moms better than the dads.

After a bit more chit-chat, lunch was delivered and we set up on the deck. The breeze was cool, but the sunshine was amazing after a long, cold winter, and the kids were having too much fun to make them clean up and go inside.

As the kids grazed on food between trips up and down the slide, Debbie explained that all the beds had new sheets, the bathrooms were stocked, and we should help ourselves to anything in the kitchen.

"If you guys will clean up, we'll head to the other house with the kids. They can play until they're exhausted, take naps, and then play again. We'll do our own little campfire before bath time and a bedtime movie later tonight. You guys are on your own for food, supplies, whatever you need for your bonfire. We'll only call you if there's an issue we can't handle—but don't expect to hear from us. We raised the three of you without too many issues, we should be fine with your angels." Debbie picked up Cori and tickled her.

Bode scoffed. "Angels, right."

Sage elbowed him. "To be fair, all of our kids are really pretty good. I've seen some monsters. I bet Gabe can vouch for them."

I held up a hand. "Believe me, your kids are absolute saints compared to some of the little demons I see in the office. Yours have manners, know the rules, and know that you are their parents not their buddies. I'd take all four of your kids over some of the patients any day."

"Exactly," Janet chimed in. "Now, let's gather the crew and head over to my place. I've got a similar sand table just for Cori."

The kids were excited to go see a different playset, and quickly gave us hugs while running toward Kyson's childhood home.

"Well, it appears they are as happy to have a night away from us as we are," Bay mused.

Bode took the kids' bags over to Janet's while the rest of us took our bags inside and moved the vehicles.

"Rhys and I will take the pull-out couch just so it's easier to let the dogs in and out," Benji said and tossed their bags on the sofa.

"I'm not sleeping in my aunt's bed," Kyson said. "We'll sleep in the basement. It's sound proof, right?" He winked.

"Well, I'm definitely not getting hot and heavy in my *mom's* bed," Bode grumbled as he came back from his delivery. "We'll take the spare room."

I glanced at Danny. "Guess we're in the big bed."

He shrugged. "Clean sheets, I've got no issues."

"Chase and Xan are planning to sleep in the bed of my truck in the barn. Something about wanting to rough it." Bode rolled his eyes. "But they're bringing an air mattress to put in the back, I don't call that roughing it. I think they just want to fuck in the barn."

"I remember some good times in that barn," Sage teased as he slapped Bode's ass. "What about Vic and Ty?"

"They said they'd bring an air mattress and put it in Mom's craft room. There's not a ton of room, but Ty has *no* interest in sleeping outside so it will have to do."

"I'm totally with Ty on that one." I shuddered. "Sleeping outside is not my idea of fun."

We spent a bit putting drinks in a cooler of ice, prepping food for later, and gathering wood for the fire. Once we'd grabbed chairs and placed them by the large pile of wood, we were free to do whatever we wanted. It was kinda weird being away from work, no chores, none of our normal to-do lists.

"Let's pull the ping-pong table outside and play for a while. We can wait to ride horses and the four-wheelers until the guys get here or ride now and later," Benji said.

"I say we ride now and later," Kyson suggested.

"Oh lord, please no horses," Rhys begged.

"You'll be fine. It wasn't the horse that caused your problem last time, you fell in the water and busted your ass," Benji teased.

We spent an hour or so playing ping-pong. It turned out the Silver crew was highly competitive and very serious about ping-pong. It also turned out that Danny and I had zero skills in the game.

Then we learned how to saddle the horses—with Bode, Benji, and Kyson doing most of the work. The only time I'd ever ridden a horse was at a county fair when I spent my tickets on a pony ride at the age of six. The horses at the Silver farm were much larger, but very gentle. I enjoyed the ride, even if I was a bit tense. Danny looked as scared on a horse as he did every time Cori wanted him to hold her—which seemed kinda strange since he had no issue with climbing on a four-hundred-pound motorcycle. But he seemed to have fun.

Bode, Benji, and Kyson showed us how to brush down the horses, unsaddle them, and give them food and water before we headed to the garage to check out the ATV selection. Helmets were distributed and we piled on four of the vehicles.

Four-wheelers were definitely more Danny's speed and I loved every second of riding on the machine behind him. It was similar to riding on the motorcycle, but the off-road aspect was a different kind of rush. I took my turn driving while Danny whooped behind me, but I preferred to be the passenger.

A couple hours later, we drove back to one of the barns, hosed off the muddy four-wheelers, and laughed at how filthy we'd gotten.

"Probably should wash up a bit," Bay suggested.

With three showers in the house and all of us very willing to double up to *save water and time*, we jumped into the showers and made the most of our time. Danny and I washed quickly, making sure to get the mud from our hair, and jacked each other off while kissing slowly as the water pelted us.

Benji and Rhys got the best end of the deal by offering to go last—they were very late joining us outside.

Vic, Ty, Chase, and Xan showed up just in time to help us load up the food and carry it out to the wood pile. Soon, we had a roaring fire, drinks in hand, and hot dogs to roast.

We spent the evening drinking, eating, laughing, and telling stories.

I loved listening to Bode and Sage talk about how they got together. Benji's and Rhys's story was one of those *truth is stranger than fiction* type tales. Kyson's and Bay's story was probably the funniest simply because Millie was highly involved in getting them together. Any time a couple has their start because of a grandma and a dildo it's going to be hilarious.

Chase and Xan were happy and content to be living together and neither had plans to make any huge changes any time soon. From what I'd heard of their lives before they found each other, it seemed they were glad to just have each other and be in a stable situation. Chase was enjoying every moment he had left with Ginny and adored any time he got to spend with Rosie. I couldn't see them ever moving away as long as Chase's sister was in Indy.

Ty and Vic surprised us all with news they were moving to California for at least a year. My heart ached to think we'd lose our friends, but I was thrilled for Ty. He'd landed an internship with a major theater production company. The internship was for twelve months, so they'd reassess at the end of that time.

"I vote we simply switch our Disney vacay from Florida to California," Kyson suggested.

With a glance around the fire, we all nodded in agreement.

By the time the night wound down—well, it was more the morning at that point—we packed up any of the perishables, doused the fire, and trooped inside, saying goodbye to Chase and Xan as they headed toward the barn.

Rhys and Benji stayed outside to make sure the dogs peed one last time. Bay and Kyson headed downstairs. Bode and Sage disappeared down the hall to the guest room and I swore I heard Sage squeal the moment the door closed behind them. Vic and Ty laughed as they closed the door to their room for the night.

Danny and I chuckled, shaking our heads as we headed down the hall to the master bedroom.

"Is it rude to have sex in the host's bed?" Danny's growly whisper against my neck as he pushed me against the door caught me off guard and turned me on.

"Well, the sheets are clean." I dropped my head to the side and moaned as he kissed my neck and nibbled the sensitive skin. "We can strip the bed on Sunday morning and be sure we put on new sheets. No one has to know."

"I plan on making sure anyone within earshot knows," Danny teased as he ran his tongue along the edge of my ear.

"Eh, they'll all be so busy they won't have time to listen to what we're doing."

We stripped out of our smoky clothes, washed off the fire smell in the shower, and fell into the fresh, clean bed. Half an hour later, Danny had made good on his promise to make sure anyone within earshot could hear us, and we collapsed into a sweaty, breathless heap.

"You're so loud," he teased.

"You're just too good." I shrugged and kissed his chest.

After we'd cleaned up, Danny pulled me into his arms and kissed me. "Move in with me," he said out of the blue.

I popped my head up. "Say what?"

"I mean it. Move in with me. My place is slightly bigger. You can move your stuff into mine or sell what you don't want." He pulled back and looked me in the eye. "If you want. No pressure if you're not on the same page, I just love having you in my bed, in my arms. Love waking up with you, falling asleep with you. Want you there, with me."

"You're okay with my work schedule?"

"Of course, we've already got that pretty much figured out. It works fine." Danny brushed a hand through my hair.

"You don't mind that I'll want to go on a cleaning spree after the end of every long shift?"

"No way. I'll clean while you're working, but you're welcome to clean any damn time you please."

"Here's the biggest one," I cocked my head to the side and waggled my brows, "can you deal with my lacy panties hanging around your place to dry after lingerie laundry day?"

"They'll look amazing hanging next to *mine*," Danny whispered before pressing a kiss to my lips. "So, what do you say? Want to make it official and move in?"

I couldn't stop the huge grin that filled my face. "Definitely, I'm all in."

THE END

Want to know more about the Silver guys? Check out Silver in the City at getbook.at/SilverCity and read their stories in Silver & Sage, Silver & Gold, and Silver & Spice.

Read more from A.D. Ellis at author.to/ADEllisAmazon

All of the places in the story are real businesses in Indy (most are *on* or at least near Mass. Ave.)

The Garden Table https://thegardentable.com
Pumkinfish https://pumkinfish.com/
Global Gifts https://www.globalgiftsft.com/
Decorate https://decorateindy.com/
Homespun https://www.homespunindy.com/

Indy Reads Books http://www.indyreadsbooks.org/

Silver in the City https://www.silverinthecity.com/

The Best Chocolate in Town https://www. bestchocolateintown.com/

Mass. Ave. Wine http://massavewine.com/

Ash & Elm https://www.ashandelmcider.com/

16-Bit Arcade http://www.16-bitbar.com/indy

If you'd like to know more about the organizations mentioned in the story or how you can donate to their causes, check out the following links:

Leukemia and Lymphoma Society https://www.lls.org/

St. Jude's Children's Hospital https://www.stjude.org/

Riley Children's Hospital https://www. rileychildrens.org/

ALSO BY A.D. ELLIS

Silver in the City (3 books- meet the Silver crew you read about in Forged in the City)

The BJ Boys Series (3 books, small town, big love)

Forever Better Together (friends to lovers)

His Reluctant Cowboy (age gap, opposites attract, cowboy romance)

What Blooms Beneath (LGBT Fantasy romance)

Sawyer

(this was the first M/M I wrote and you may remember Sawyer and Luke being mentioned in Barrett & Ivan as well as in Ryker & Gavin)

* * *

Start Something About Him with a **FREE** short story:

(The Beginning https://instafreebie.com/free/84Cxr)

Then continue with the other stand-alone titles in the series (available to read FREE for Kindle Unlimited subscribers):

Bryan & Jase

Brody & Nick

Barrett & Ivan

Braeton & Drew

Ryker & Gavin

Kade & Cameron

Or grab the boxset HERE.

* * *

Plus several other titles:

Devoted (a Something About Him novella)

Saving Us

Stranded Hearts (a short story)

Eli & Gage (a Something About Him short story)

* * *

A.D.'s first stories (all male/female except Sawyer which is male/male) are in the Torey Hope and Torey Hope: The Later Years series. Find the 8 book box set HERE or you can find each individual title on Amazon.

For Nicky

Because of Beckett

Christmas in Torey Hope

Loving Josie

Decker

Sawyer

Zach

Kendrick

ABOUT THE AUTHOR

A.D. Ellis is an Indiana girl, born and raised. She spends much of her time in central Indiana as an instructional coach/teacher in the inner city of Indianapolis, being a mom to two amazing school-aged children, and wondering how she and her husband of almost two decades have managed to not drive each other insane. A lot of her time is also devoted to phone call avoidance and her hatred of cooking.

She loves chocolate, wine, pizza, and naps along with reading and writing romance. These loves don't leave much time for housework, much to the chagrin of her husband. Who would pick cleaning the house over a nap or a good book? She uses any extra time to increase her fluency in sarcasm.

Find all of Ellis' contemporary romance and male/male romance at www.adellisauthor.com

FREE books-- sign up at bit.ly/ADEllisNews for a FREE male/female romance.

Sign up at http://www.subscribepage.com/ADEllisNewsMMRomance for a FREE male/male romance book.

ACKNOWLEDGMENTS

It's always so hard to write this part because I'm worried I'll forget someone without meaning to.

Readers- you are the reason I write. As long as you continue reading my stories, I'll continue writing them. Thank you for your support.

Bloggers- your support, reviews, and promotion are very much appreciated. Thank you!

My author buddies- I don't know that I could keep doing this without our brainstorm sessions, laughter, road trips, meals, wine, and friendship as my support.

Thank you to my alphas, betas, editors, proofreaders, and ARC readers! Your eyes and input are beyond important to me.

Brett and Gage- as usual, I doubt you even grasp how much your support, input, and friendship mean to me. This author journey has brought many wonderful things into my life, and you both are two of the BEST! I'm blessed to call you friends.

My family and friends- thank you for your love and support, always.